"I didn't have an alibi."

Logan's voice was low and carefully neutral as he explained the facts to Marilee.

"That shouldn't mean—"

"I was twenty, Marilee, and I'd sowed a lot of wild oats by that time. The good people of Newellton figured it was better to get me off the streets as soon as possible. I was just lucky hanging was out of fashion."

"But the guilty person went free."

"Yeah, I noticed." He wished he'd had a woman by his side back then, with Marilee's absolute confidence that they'd gotten the wrong guy. Maybe it would have made a difference if someone had cared. Maybe they'd have looked just a little harder for the right guy.

His gaze settled on Marilee's lips. The lower one was slightly full, naturally sensuous. He'd wanted to bed her since the moment she'd entered his house. But for now, he'd settle for a kiss. One kiss. It had been so damn long....

Dear Reader;

Silhouette Romance begins the New Year with six heartwarming stories of the enduring power of love. Felicity Burrow thought she would never trust her heart again—until she met Lucas Carver and his darling little boy in *A Father's Vow*, this month's FABULOUS FATHER by favorite author Elizabeth August.

Love comes when least expected in Carolyn Zane's *The Baby Factor*, another irresistible BUNDLES OF JOY. Elaine Lewis was happy to marry Brent Clark— temporarily, of course. It was the one way to keep her unborn baby. What she didn't bet on was falling in love!

Karen Rose Smith's emotional style endures in *Shane's Bride*. Nothing surprised Shane Walker more than when Hope Franklin walked back into his life with a little boy she claimed was his. Loving little Christopher was easy, but trusting Hope again would prove a lot harder. Could Hope manage to regain Shane's trust and, more important, his love?

The sparks fly fast and furiously in Charlotte Moore's *The Maverick Takes a Wife*. When Logan Spurwood fought to clear his name, Marilee Haggerty couldn't resist helping him in his search for the truth. Soon she yearned to help him find strength in her love, as well….

And two couples discover whirlwind romance in Natalie Patrick's *The Marriage Chase* and *His Secret Son* by debut author Betty Jane Sanders.

Happy Reading!

Anne Canadeo

Please address questions and book requests to:
Silhouette Reader Service
U.S.: 3010 Walden Ave., P.O. Box 1325, Buffalo, NY 14269
Canadian: P.O. Box 609, Fort Erie, Ont. L2A 5X3

THE MAVERICK TAKES A WIFE

Charlotte Moore

Silhouette
ROMANCE™

Published by Silhouette Books

America's Publisher of Contemporary Romance

SILHOUETTE BOOKS

ISBN 0-373-19129-4

THE MAVERICK TAKES A WIFE

Printed in U.S.A.

Books by Charlotte Moore

Silhouette Romance

Not the Marrying Kind #975
Belated Bride #1088
The Maverick Takes a Wife #1129

CHARLOTTE MOORE

has always enjoyed putting words on paper. Until recently most of these words have been nonfiction, including a weekly newspaper column that has recruited nearly twenty thousand volunteers in the past twenty years for some four hundred different local nonprofit organizations.

When she is not urging people to get involved in their community, Charlotte divides her time among writing, volunteering for her favorite organizations (including Orange County Chapter of Romance Writers of America), trying *not* to mother two married daughters and sharing her life in Southern California with her own special hero, Chuck.

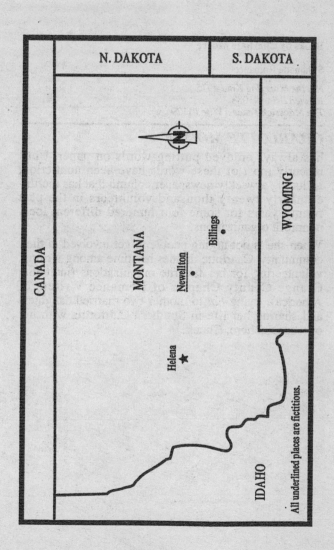

N. DAKOTA

S. DAKOTA

CANADA

MONTANA

WYOMING

Billings

Newellton

Helena

IDAHO

All underlined places are fictitious.

Chapter One

Marilee blasted the car horn three times, long and loud. For the past thirty minutes she'd been trying to attract someone's attention. Sliding off the road and getting stuck in a snowdrift hadn't been on her travel itinerary. Nor did she like the idea of putting her son, Glen, at risk in a blizzard by trying to walk back to the ranch house she'd glimpsed through the blowing snow a few minutes before they'd gone into the ditch. In this kind of weather, a person could get lost and freeze only feet away from safety. It was better to stay in the car.

With a silent prayer, she hit the horn again.

An instant later, she had to stifle the startled scream that rose in her throat as someone tapped loudly on the window.

"Hey, lady, are you okay in there?"

"Yes, yes. We're fine." Shaken, but relieved beyond belief that someone had finally come to their rescue, Marilee Haggerty gave her son a brave smile. "See, I told you someone would hear our horn."

"Yeah, Mom. But we've been stuck here a long time. I was kinda getting scared."

"I know, honey, but everything will be fine now." She lowered the side window a crack. An icy blast of wind drove pebbly snowflakes inside to sting her face. "Do you think you could pull us out of the ditch? We're already overdue at our destination."

"You're not going anywhere in this blizzard, even if I could haul your car out of that drift. None of the roads are plowed. You'd better get whatever you need and I'll take you to my place. It's not far."

In any other circumstances, Marilee wouldn't have gone off anywhere with a stranger, certainly not one who looked just this side of scruffy.

But waiting out the storm in the car wasn't an option. She knew spring blizzards in Montana could unexpectedly race down from the Arctic with a blast of cold air, to bury the landscape in winter white just when you'd started hoping for a break in the weather. She'd simply been caught unaware. This was a long way from the benign climate she'd grown used to in Los Angeles. But then, it wasn't the warm sunshine she was escaping by returning north. She wanted to create a home for her thirteen-year-old son, one where he wouldn't be faced with the daily threat of violence simply by going to school. Returning to the state where she'd been born seemed a logical place to begin a new life.

"Come on, Glen, let's get our suitcases out of the back." She popped the trunk lid and shoved her door open against the howling wind. The canted angle of the car made getting out awkward.

"Watch your step," the stranger ordered, firmly gripping Marilee's elbow before her feet slipped out from under her. He was a big man, she realized, with a roughly textured voice. As she bent her head to avoid the pelting snow, she got a view of long legs and muscular thighs encased in blue denim, and scuffed cowboy boots that had seen better days.

"I'm certainly glad you found us," she shouted over the noise of the wind.

"If I hadn't gone to check on the horses in the barn, I wouldn't have heard the horn. What are you doing out in this mess, anyway?"

"I took the wrong turn off the highway."

"Nobody should be on the road today. Don't you listen to the weather reports?"

"When you have a thirteen year-old son, you listen to rock music." Marilee's voice was wry and resigned.

She heard a low, rumbling sound that could have been the storm, but was more likely a laugh from the man escorting her to the back of the car.

Lifting the trunk lid, she pulled a duffel bag out of the crammed compartment and gave it to Glen. "You need anything else?" she asked.

"Naw." He patted his jacket pocket. "I got my ears."

"Terrific." Her son was rarely without the earphones that linked him to the nearest rock-music station and helped him avoid anything resembling an intelligent conversation with his mother.

Hefting her suitcase, she handed it to the stranger. His eyes were the color of pewter rain clouds, she noted, his jaw shadowed by dark whiskers.

He grunted under the weight of the luggage. "Bricks, right?"

Suppressing an amused smile, she checked the trunk to see what else she might need for an overnight stay, selecting a small backpack she used for a makeup kit. "Most of our things are in storage for now."

"I think my back—and your shock absorbers—are grateful for that small blessing." He reached up to close the trunk. "Come on. Let's get out of here before we freeze our buns."

He helped her through foot-deep snow to his truck, a four-wheel-drive pickup with dented fenders, oversize snow tires and a cracked windshield. He tossed her suitcase into the back, along with Glen's duffel, and Marilee climbed into a deliciously warm cab.

"You okay, hon?" she asked Glen as he slid in beside her.

"Yeah, I'm fine, Mom. No sweat."

She found herself squeezed between her son and the stranger. "I'm Marilee Haggerty, and this is Glen."

"Luke Spurwood." He shifted into gear, and the tires spun before grabbing. The windshield wipers struggled valiantly against the fast-falling snow as he executed a U-turn and headed back down the narrow country road. Only the faint indentation of tire tracks on the opposite side of the road showed that anyone had traveled this way, and the tracks were filling fast.

"Your ranch must be the one we passed a while ago," she said. With their thighs pressed together, Marilee was acutely aware of her rescuer's size, his unkempt whiskers and the shaggy black hair that reached the collar of his sheepskin coat. In Los Angeles, she would have had more sense than to get into any vehicle with a man like this, never mind his ruggedly handsome profile. Here, in the middle of a blizzard, she'd had little choice.

"Ranch's about a quarter mile, but it's hard to spot in this storm."

"I hope your wife doesn't object to unexpected visitors." With the snow falling so hard, there was no telling how long Marilee and her son would be stuck out here in ranch country.

"No wife. I live alone."

Marilee swallowed the "oh" that formed on her lips. Luke Spurwood was probably the most masculine man she'd ever met—dangerously so. Yet he didn't have a wife. Finding herself en route to his remote ranch on a snow-blown Montana prairie would make any woman nervous, she told herself. Fortunately, she had Glen for a chaperon. And maybe luck would be with her and the storm would clear in a hurry.

Turning off the road through an almost indistinguishable break in the wire fence, Luke headed the truck across open country. Blowing snow mounded against stray clumps of sagebrush and cut the visibility to a minimum. A structure emerged from the gloom like a ghostly apparition. The truck stopped near the entrance.

Even through the blizzard, Marilee could see that the ranch house was run down. The front porch sagged at a weary angle and paint was peeling on the clapboard siding.

An anxious feeling fluttered in the pit of her stomach. She hoped she and her son hadn't escaped the danger of freezing to death in their car only to end up in a situation far more perilous.

Trouble had showed up on Luke's doorstep.

He sensed it in Marilee's sultry scent, something subtle that had played on his nerves in the truck. When she stepped into his living room and shrugged out of her heavy jacket, he knew he didn't need this kind of grief. She was trouble with a capital *T* for a man who hadn't had a glimpse of a woman like her on anything other than a girlie calendar for eight long years.

Maybe she wasn't the most beautiful woman in the world. She had a nose that turned up a little too much and was dotted with freckles, and a pair of lips that were a bit too full. But on the other hand she had a knockout, break-your-heart, pinup figure, generous where it needed to be and slim and trim in between. She was the kind of woman men bragged about in locker rooms and sweated about in their dreams. Luke didn't need any of that.

He should have ignored that damn horn she'd been honking. Rescuing a damsel in distress—with her teenage kid in tow—wasn't part of his game plan. Now he was stuck with seeing the play through.

"You want some coffee or something to warm you up?" he asked.

She rubbed her hands together, slender fingers shiny with clear polish at the tips. A woman's hands. Gentle hands. And no wedding ring.

"That'd be nice, but I don't want you to go to any bother."

"No bother. It's only instant." He turned to the boy, whose nose matched his mother's, freckles included. Mother and son both had hair that looked like it had been touched by a rosy Montana sunrise, except the boy's was wild with cowlicks and hers was tied back in a tight bun that Luke had the urge to unleash. "You want something, Glen?"

The kid shrugged. "A soda, if you've got it."

Polite. That was nice in a kid these days. "I'll show you the rooms upstairs you can use and then I'll check what's in the fridge and start the hot water going."

"We appreciate your hospitality," Marilee said.

Luke suspected she'd probably appreciate it less if she knew what thoughts had been going through his head. And she'd be right. Rumpled sheets and sweaty bodies—hers, his—shouldn't be on his mind.

"I don't get many visitors. The ranch is kind of isolated."

Isolated. As Marilee followed Luke up the stairs, the word shimmered through her self-protective barriers like a keening wind slips through a crack in mortar. A shiver traveled down her spine. "How far is it to the next ranch?"

"We're pretty spread out in this part of the country. A couple of miles, I suppose. Maybe more."

She'd suspected as much. Too far to run for help, particularly in a raging snowstorm. "It must be lonely."

"It used to bother me as a kid. It doesn't anymore."

"My mom was born in Montana," Glen announced from the back of the small parade. "We're gonna go see her sister in Newellton. She's got a new baby."

Luke paused at the top of the stairs and turned. "You *did* take a wrong turn. By about twenty miles' worth."

"That far?" Marilee asked. Lord, he looked big when he stood above her on the next higher step. Big and intimidating, in a wool shirt with an open collar and sleeves rolled up to show muscular forearms sprinkled with dark hair.

"Give or take a quarter mile or so."

"I haven't been in Montana for a long time. I guess I got confused with the highway off ramps."

"Visibility was probably bad."

"Dismal. And I was pushing it to get to Newellton, in spite of the weather," she admitted. "Not too smart of me."

The gaze of his pewter eyes swept over her face, then dipped lower, lingering on the rise and fall of her breasts beneath her heavy wool sweater. "Anybody can make a mistake."

Marilee had made her fair share of mistakes, but getting stranded in the middle of a blizzard with a gray-eyed, darkly dangerous man counted right up there with the worst of them. "Maybe I could call my sister to let her know we're okay. She'll be worried."

"Sorry. There's no phone."

Her jaw dropped. What kind of a man didn't own a phone? A hermit? Or, more ominously, one who had something to hide?

"There's no power, either. The lines are down everywhere. The lights are working off a generator."

Before Marilee had a chance to register relief that it was the storm that made Luke appear to be a hermit, he turned, and with a few long-legged strides, reached a doorway. There was a sense of contained energy about him, along with a certain haunted wariness that she'd seen in his eyes.

"This oughta do for you, Glen," he said, shoving open a bedroom door.

"Great." Glen lugged his duffel bag inside.

Marilee peered after him. The room was starkly furnished, with a single bed, a desk and one chest of drawers. Faded patches on the old wallpaper suggested every memento or picture that had once adorned the walls had been ripped off and never replaced, as though the owner had wanted to rid himself of the memories.

"Your mom can stay across the hall," Luke announced.

Following his gesture, Marilee entered a room that could have been bright and cheerful, except the drapes were drawn across the windows and there was a general musty smell about the place. The dark furniture was old and worn, but the double bed looked reasonably comfortable.

Setting her suitcase on the floor, Luke said, "I'll have to round up some clean sheets and stuff for both of you. There ought to be enough blankets on the beds."

"We'll be fine," Marilee assured him. He was too big for the room, too overpowering with his long, shaggy hair and dark good looks. At some very deep level, she found Luke Spurwood more than just a physical threat. Intuitively she knew he had the ability to slip inside the emotional space she'd so carefully protected for the last fourteen years. Stiffening under his intense scrutiny, she vowed not to let that happen.

"I sleep downstairs, so I don't usually heat the whole place. It'll be cold for a while till the furnace gets up to speed."

"It's better than freezing in the car," she said with feeling.

They were standing three or four feet apart, but Marilee felt an electric current arcing between them in the silence—one stronger than the static electricity that comes with dry winter air, and far more potent. It was crazy that she'd feel that way, when Luke Spurwood basically scared her to death. Particularly when they were standing in a bedroom, with all its erotic implications.

Luke cleared his throat. "I'll go fire up the hot water for coffee." Whirling, he left the room.

Only then did Marilee expel the breath she'd been holding.

* * *

Marilee wrapped her hands around her coffee mug. In spite of the heater humming down in the basement, the house felt cold, and the wind kept rattling the kitchen windows as the darkness of evening fell early.

Luke stood looking out into the deepening twilight. A frown tugged his brows into a straight line. "Before this storm started, the cows had begun to drop their calves." His voice was low, almost as though he was talking to his own reflection in the rippled windowpane.

"This cold weather can't be good for newborns."

"Nature doesn't always take that little detail into account. And if the temperature drops any more, none of the calves will make it."

"Do you have a big herd?"

He shifted his attention back to the kitchen, his gray eyes troubled. "No. And I can't afford to lose a single head."

"Hey, Luke," Glen called, coming into the kitchen with the loose-legged saunter of adolescents. "I can't find your TV."

"Must be because I don't have one. We're too far out from Helena to pick up a decent signal."

Glen looked at him dumbly. "But you've got a satellite dish, or cable or something, don't you? I wanted to watch MTV."

"Sorry. No dish. No cable. No MTV." Luke leaned back against the kitchen counter and folded his arms. A faint smile played at the corners of his lips.

"No?" Glen echoed. He acted as though Luke was speaking in a foreign language, which was probably true for the boy.

"Well, you've got a stereo, right?" he persisted, a little desperately. "Some CDs? See, my ears aren't picking up anything but a news station. Really boring stuff."

"That's how it is out here. Boring."

"I'm sure you can manage without TV for one night, Glen," Marilee admonished.

"But there isn't even any music on the radio," he protested. "Just some country-western stuff, and that doesn't even count. What am I supposed to do?"

"I think there're some games in the front closet," Luke suggested.

"Games?"

"You know. Monopoly, Scrabble—that kind of game."

Glen's lip curled in disdain. "That's kid stuff."

"Yep." Luke shoved away from the counter. He remembered well enough what it was like to be a teenager on a ranch a long way from town. Mostly backbreaking work and loneliness. Now he appreciated the solitude, though he had no intention of making a career on this poor piece of the prairie that grew more rocks than grass.

As soon as he could take care of some unsettled business in Newellton, he was going to sell the ranch and what poor livestock he could lay title to. Then he'd be gone. His life had been on hold too long already.

"You can help me bed down the horses in the barn and check the generator," he suggested to Glen.

"He doesn't have any cold-weather boots," Marilee interjected. "I didn't see any point in buying him a pair, not when he outgrows shoes in about two months and this is supposed to be springtime. Even in Montana."

"There's an extra pair of boots on the service porch that ought to come close to fitting." He eyed the boy. "*If* you want to come along, Glen."

The youth shrugged. "I guess. There's nothin' else worth doin' around here."

Marilee seemed to hesitate, and Luke could tell the mind of an overprotective mother was at work. He guessed she had the right to be concerned, these days, but she was going to have to learn to let the kid go.

"Well, all right," she said, surprising Luke with her agreement. "But you'll see that he doesn't wander off in this weather? He's not used to the cold."

"Geez, Mom, I'm not a little kid."

Her eyes were more green than blue, Luke decided, and at the moment they were filled with concern. A man would appreciate knowing a woman like her was worrying about him. He couldn't remember the last time anyone had given a damn about him.

"I've got a tension line strung between the house and the barn in case the wind or the visibility gets too bad. He won't get lost," he assured her.

Her smile was less than enthusiastic, but she nodded her approval. "If you tell me what's on the menu, I'll start dinner while you're out in the barn."

"There's some ground meat in the freezer. Whatever you want to stir up will be fine. I'm not a fussy eater."

He headed for the back porch and his coat, Glen shuffling along right behind him.

When Marilee called after her son, "Button up good," Luke found himself wishing her admonition had been meant for him.

When he'd helped Glen prepare for the cold and the two of them had stepped outside, Luke pulled his collar up and ducked his head against the blowing wind. The mercury had inched down several degrees. Not a good sign. Colder temperatures meant more trouble. If the weather didn't ease, he'd have to go out in the morning to look for any calves that had been dropped and make sure they were in sheltered places. It was a hell of a thing for a blizzard to hit so late in the year.

A horse nickered as he stepped into the barn, and the air was thick with the scents of hay and manure. Luke could still see his breath fog in front of his face. There were cracks in the barn siding and a half-dozen leaks in the roof. The bank had been managing the ranch for the past six months, since Luke's father had died. They hadn't done a hell of a lot better job than his drunken old man.

"You okay, Glen?" he asked, closing the door behind the boy.

"Sure is cold out there."

"Wait till August. It'll warm up." He handed Glen a pitchfork. "Where are you and your mom from?"

"L.A."

"Your dad live there, too?" Luke asked the question casually, as if the answer didn't matter one way or the other. He forked some straw into a stall.

The boy did the same, a little awkward with the unfamiliar tool. "I don't have a father. But if you're planning to hit on my mother, I gotta warn you she doesn't date much."

"That so?" Luke wondered why, then realized it didn't matter. He hardly had enough spare change to buy Marilee a hamburger, much less consider asking her out on a real date. But perversely, he was relieved to confirm that there was no husband or boyfriend in the picture—even though he knew, when she learned the truth, Marilee wouldn't give him the time of day.

Marilee looked up as a blast of cold air preceded Luke and Glen into the kitchen. Her son's cheeks were pink with cold, and both men were smiling, as though they'd been laughing over some masculine joke. Marilee knew Glen needed to have male role models. She just wasn't sure Luke was the ideal candidate for the job. But maybe men who lived alone always looked a little rough around the edges.

"Dinner will be ready in about a half hour," she said. "I made a chili-cheese casserole. Hope that's okay."

"It smells great. Lots better than what I'd fix for myself." Luke ran his palm over his stubbled jaw. "I'll go clean up before we eat."

"Hey, Mom, did ya know Luke's got an old Harley out in the barn? A three-hundred-cc job that he stripped and put back together again when he was a kid. Neat, huh?"

"Wonderful, I'm sure."

Glen snatched a piece of bread from the table and bit into it.

"You go wash up, too, young man. And no snacking before dinner."

"Yeah, right, Mom." He swaggered out of the kitchen in a fair imitation of Luke's long, muscular stride.

A few minutes later she heard water running, and about the time she was going to call dinner, she heard laughter from the living room. She went to the doorway to check what was happening.

Marilee drew in a quick breath. Luke had showered and shaved, his neatly combed hair now damp at his collar. He looked suddenly more youthful, but no less rugged, with a square jaw and sensuous lips. His head was bent close to Glen's as they concentrated on a hand-held, electronic football game, a relic from his youth retrieved from the closet, Marilee suspected. The contrast between the two of them was striking, with Luke so dark and Marilee's son so fair—like midnight and sunrise.

"I gotta throw a pass, man," Glen insisted. "It's third and about twenty."

"A quarterback draw—that's the perfect play. The defense will be expecting a pass."

"No way, man. I'm gonna pass."

The electronic box beeped and dinged, both men watching intently.

"Oh, no!" Glen groaned. He slammed his fist down on his knee.

"Interception! I told you they'd be waiting for a pass." Luke slapped the boy on his back. "Too bad, kid. That's the game. But you'll get 'em next time."

Something went all tight and achy inside Marilee. Glen needed a man in his life who knew something about football, a man who could counter what she knew was her tendency to hover. And she needed someone, too. The possibility of that kind of a commitment, of being vulnerable in that kind of a relationship, had terrified her for a long time. But maybe, for Glen's sake, she ought to make the effort to put her fears aside.

"You two ready to take a break for dinner?" she asked, her voice more husky with emotion than she would have liked.

Luke looked up, a little startled, as though he had forgotten she was in the house—or was embarrassed to be caught playing a kid's game with such enthusiasm. When he gave her a half smile, that achy feeling inside Marilee settled a little lower in her body, making her terribly aware of just how long it had been since she'd allowed herself to pay attention to her own needs or to care about anyone other than her son.

Somehow she managed to get the dinner served. She ate almost mechanically, all the time trying not to think about the shape of Luke's tapered fingers as he held a knife to spread butter on his bread, or the breadth of his shoulders as he sat across the table from her. She didn't participate much in the conversation, which centered on the Rams and Seahawks, running backs and wide receivers. But she was intensely aware of the deep timbre of Luke's voice and how the vibrations from it spread like fingers of warm honey down her spine.

When they'd finished with dinner, Glen excused himself, intent on returning to the electronic football game. Luke stayed to help with cleanup and the dishes.

"Your son's a good kid. He hasn't exactly mastered a pitchfork yet, but he did fine helping with the chores." Dribbling detergent into the sink, Luke ran the hot water. "It can't be easy raising a boy alone."

"We manage okay. But there are days..." She shrugged. "Thirteen isn't the best age in the world."

A smile kicked up the corner of his mouth. "I can imagine. I wasn't exactly a saint myself when I was a kid."

Nor had Marilee been the perfect adolescent, she silently admitted. Far from it. And the whole town of Newellton had been aware of her transgressions—both real and imagined. She'd made the mistake of thinking the attention of a boy, almost any boy—and the sex he was interested in—was the same as love. It had taken her a long time to discover her error. By then she was the talk of the town and her reputation outstripped even her wildest imagination.

"We weren't living in a real good neighborhood in L.A., and I started worrying. There was some gang activity in his school."

"In junior high?"

"Awful, isn't it? They're all so young, so set on ruining their lives before they even get started." She took a plate he'd washed and ran the dish towel around it. Though the kitchen lacked some modern amenities, it was a pleasant room with oak cabinets and a white tile counter. "Anyway, I decided it might be a better environment if we moved back here, to Montana."

"Permanently?"

"I've got a job lined up in Helena, in the city planning department."

"I thought you were visiting your sister."

"We are, or we're supposed to be, except for the storm. I don't have to be in Helena for a few weeks. I figured it wouldn't be the end of the world if Glen missed some school. He's a pretty bright kid."

"Like his mom?"

She felt heat color her cheeks. "I'm not sure where he gets his brains." Though she doubted Glen's intelligence came from his father. She'd made a very bad choice in that regard, which she'd tried to write off as youthful folly. Or the special confusion of a young girl whose own father had died, leaving her feeling abandoned. So while she'd been eager to return to her Montana roots, she'd never considered making her home in Newellton again. The memories were simply too painful.

Reestablishing contact with her sister, Beth, after nearly fourteen years of silence was as close as Marilee wanted her ties to Newellton to be.

Luke rinsed off the silverware and placed it on the drain board. "Sorry there's no way you can get a hold of your sister to let her know you're okay."

"The storm can't last forever. But I wasn't too smart getting off the highway onto the wrong road. I imagine by now Beth's husband has sent out an all-points bulletin for us.''

''He's the nervous type?''

''Not that I know of. But he is the County Sheriff. You've probably heard of him. Raymond Hawk?''

''I don't think so.'' His hands paused over the casserole dish he'd been scrubbing. ''I've been away for a long time. Eight years.''

''Really? Why?''

''I've been in prison.'' He said it slowly, distinctly, as though he didn't want there to be any misunderstanding.

Marilee almost dropped the glass she'd been drying. ''Jail? What did you do?'' She blurted the question, as half-formed hopes and dreams shattered into a thousand sharp-edged shards in the face of reality. Fear sliced through her.

He turned to looked at her, his steely gray eyes hard and haunted. ''Some people called it murder.''

Chapter Two

Myriad emotions played across Marilee's face in a kaleidoscope of vividly painful expressions: shock, horror, then a growing sense of fear. She took a step back.

Luke cursed himself. He never should have laid the news on her so bluntly. What bitter irony that the woman who had showed up on his doorstep needing his help was the sister-in-law of the sheriff. And Luke had a serious bone to pick with the law.

"I'm not a serial killer, if that's what you're afraid of. I was innocent."

Her gaze darted around the room, as if she was looking for stray bodies he might have forgotten to bury. "I suspect that's what most convicted criminals claim."

"In my case, it's true."

"Okay." Her voice hitched on the word. She nodded, though he didn't for a minute think she believed him. Most people didn't, including twelve good men and women who were supposed to have been his peers. They'd been all too eager to convict a twenty-year-old kid and salve their consciences in the process.

"I did the time and paid the price. I'm free to come and go as I please now. But I never killed anyone." He'd never be the same, though. Prison took a man's spirit and cauterized every soft feeling he had, leaving nothing but a hard, jagged scar covering the wound.

Marilee put the dried glass on the cupboard shelf where it belonged. With fear tightening her chest, she was having considerable trouble breathing. She and her son were in an isolated ranch house, in the middle of a blizzard, with a murderer. Or if not a full-fledged murderer, certainly an ex-con. The phones were out, and who knew how long the storm would last, how long they would be trapped together?

Now she understood why his gray eyes seemed so wary. She imagined that's what happened to men who had been in jail. They learned to always be on their guard.

From the living room, she heard the pinging of the football game as Glen tried to master the sport.

For the sake of her son, Marilee had to remain calm. She didn't know if Luke was a violent man, prone to emotional outbursts, or a methodical killer who stalked his prey. She didn't know a single thing for sure about Luke Spurwood, except that he'd spent time in jail for a crime he claimed not to have committed.

And, for one brief moment, she had allowed herself to feel attracted to him. Powerfully so. She hadn't permitted that kind of weakness since she'd been in high school.

Evidently her ability to judge men hadn't improved one whit with the passing years.

She nodded toward the sink. "Your soapy water is getting cold." It was an inane comment, such an ordinary observation that she saw some of the tautness leave the rigid set of Luke's shoulders. Do murderers wash dishes? she suddenly wondered. Or play electronic football games with adolescent boys?

The answers weren't important, she told herself. As long as she and her son got safely away from Luke's ranch, she'd very likely never see him again. Getting involved with a convicted criminal, whether or not he'd paid his debt to society, would be beyond foolhardy for a woman who was still haunted by her own reckless past.

"Hey, Luke," Glen called from the living room. "Aren't you through in there yet? I got this game whipped. It's a snap."

"In a minute." Luke pulled the plug from the sink and rested his big, masculine hands on the edge of the counter as he watched the water swirl down the drain. "If you want, I'll stay away from your boy."

How could Marilee demand that of a man who had rescued them from a snowdrift and offered them his hospitality?

"It's all right," she said softly. "The storm can't last too long. We'll probably be gone by tomorrow."

* * *

In the dim light of morning, Marilee hurried down the stairs and into the kitchen. She snatched up the wall phone. She'd been hoping all through a restless night that the phone would be back in working order by the time she awoke. It wasn't. There wasn't so much as a static hum on the line.

Out the window, the dawn sky was a streak of silver in a cold, cloudless sky. Maybe she and Glen could walk to—

"You're an early riser."

She nearly jumped out of her skin at the sound of Luke's deep voice.

"I didn't mean to startle you," he said, his gaze following her hand as she hurriedly cradled the phone. "The lines are still down?"

"Yes." And her heart was pumping a thousand beats a minute. She wanted to be away from here, away from Luke and the ricocheting emotions that had kept her awake half the night. She was drawn to him, fascinated by his dark good looks, and at the same time repelled by the thought of what he might have done.

"It'll be several hours before the plows make it to this part of the county. After they go by, I'll haul your car out of the drift and you can be on your way. Assuming you didn't bust anything when you went into the ditch."

"I'll appreciate that."

Her eyes locked with his for a moment. She saw bleakness in their depths this morning and the knowledge that she was afraid of him. Afraid he was a murderer. She felt the sting of guilt. He'd told her that he was innocent, but how could she know for sure? People weren't sent to jail on a whim. She definitely didn't feel safe trusting her own instincts.

He crossed the room to the stove and snapped on the burner under the teakettle. He was wearing the same wool shirt he'd had on yesterday, a faded plaid in browns and greens. It looked a little snug across the shoulders, as though his physique had filled out since it was purchased—clothing that had been bought before he went to prison.

How did a man deal with a life so regimented that he wasn't allowed to chose his own clothing?

"I'm going to go out looking for the cattle this morning," he said, "and see if any of them are in trouble. I'll try to be back by noon."

"You're going out alone?" In spite of the heavy robe she was wearing, Marilee shivered at the thought. This was definitely not a spring day on the beaches of Los Angeles.

He shrugged. "I don't exactly have a lot of hired hands around the place."

"Isn't that, well, dangerous? I mean, what happens if you run into trouble?" Marilee knew enough about ranching and Montana to know a man alone could be injured and freeze to death in weather like this before anyone was aware he needed help.

"The temperature's below zero. If any of the cows dropped their calves overnight, they'll probably freeze unless I can get them to shelter. I need every damn one of those calves if I'm going to sell the herd and the ranch and clear enough money so I can turn my back on this place for good."

"You're planning to leave?"

"You got that straight. I'm going to spend some time trying to clear my name. But even if I can't, when I sell the ranch I'm outta here. For good."

"I ran away once. It only meant I took my troubles with me."

He raised questioning eyebrows.

Before he could voice any queries, she retrieved two mugs from the cupboard and found the instant coffee. "I don't think you ought to go out in this cold alone. Isn't there a neighbor you can call to help?"

"I've been away eight years, Marilee, and only back six weeks. I don't even know who owns the next ranch anymore. What I do know is that there are cattle out there with the Spurwood brand on their flanks. I intend to stake my claim to every last one of 'em I can."

Glen wandered into the room wearing his pajamas and looking sleepy eyed. "Did I hear you're going to round up the cattle?"

"Not exactly," Luke said. "I'm just going to check on the calves."

"Can I come along?"

"No, you can't, honey. It's too cold and you—"

"Aw, Mom, I don't wanta sit around here all day. And when else am I gonna have a chance to do something like that? We're moving to some dumb city. It might be smaller than L.A. but it's still pretty big, and I bet every kid there has been on a roundup." He shot a hopeful look in Luke's direction. "Right, Luke? It'd be okay if I came along, wouldn't it?"

"It's up to your mother." Luke studiously avoided meeting Marilee's eyes by pouring the hot water into the two mugs she'd prepared.

Marilee nearly groaned aloud. She'd been had. She'd just told Luke it was too dangerous for him to go alone, but she certainly couldn't let her boy go out there in the company of a convicted killer, particularly when her son had no cold-weather experience at all and was already developing a bad case of hero worship. That would be asking for double trouble.

"You two are ganging up on me," she complained.

"All right, Mom!" Assuming she'd already conceded defeat, Glen grinned widely. "It'll take me just a minute to get dressed, Luke."

"Just hold your horses, young man. You'll eat a proper breakfast and then we'll *both* get dressed so we can help Luke."

Luke's head snapped up. "What?"

"Well, you don't think I'd let Glen go out there in this freezing weather without me, do you? He doesn't know a thing about cattle."

"And you do?"

She wasn't about to admit she'd been a town girl. So she tossed her head and said casually, "I know enough."

"I bet," he grumbled, but there was a spark of challenge in his eyes that did something quite extraordinary to Marilee's heart.

She was not, absolutely *not,* going to get involved with an ex-con! Particularly a dangerously compelling man with riveting gray eyes.

* * *

The sun glinted off the snow, creating a dazzling halo of white crystals around Luke and his horse. Marilee put on her sunglasses. Shifting the truck into low gear, she followed him away from the ranch house and out across the barren landscape. In the back of the truck, Luke had loaded bales of hay for the cattle. Assuming they could find any.

"He's a pretty neat guy, isn't he, Mom?"

She didn't need to ask who her son was talking about. "Yes, honey, he seems very nice." The nicest ex-con she'd ever come across.

"He knows a lot about football."

"I gathered as much."

"He played quarterback in high school, but he had to quit the team because his dad needed help on the ranch. Did you know he went to Newellton High?"

Her gloved fingers tightened around the steering wheel at the mention of the scene of her downfall. She hoped to get into Newellton, visit her sister for a few weeks, and get out of town again without ever meeting anyone who remembered her.

"Did you know him, Mom?"

"I don't think so, dear." She would have recalled Luke Spurwood. Worse, he probably would have recognized her. "I'd guess we were in different classes." Was he older or younger? she wondered, realizing that wary look in his eyes gave him an ageless appearance.

Luke angled toward a stand of cottonwoods, their winter-bare branches already showing signs of spring buds in spite of the snow on the ground. A group of shaggy-looking cattle huddled in the shelter of the trees. He dismounted, and Marilee stopped the truck nearby, their arrival disturbing a pair of meadowlarks from their perch in the trees.

After the relative warmth of the cab, the air felt bitterly cold. Her blood must have thinned while she'd been living in California. In contrast, Luke had been riding along in the open as if it were a summer day. A determined man, she decided.

He dragged a bale of hay off the back of the truck, cut the twine and used a rake to spread it around on the snow.

"We can help," Marilee said. "You need another bale?"

He eyed her for a moment, as though reluctant to admit there was anything he couldn't do alone, then nodded. "They're heavy."

"We'll manage."

Working together, Marilee and Glen slid the second bale out of the truck onto the ground.

Lowing contentedly, the cattle ambled out of their sheltered spot toward the waiting feed. Two newborns wobbled along beside their mothers.

"Those two little ones look healthy enough," Marilee remarked, while Luke spread the second bale.

"This group managed to get out of the wind. Not all of 'em are likely to be so smart. We'll keep looking." He shoved the tailgate closed, then remounted his chestnut gelding. He rode tall and straight, with the confidence of years spent in the saddle. Marilee found herself admiring his proud silhouette.

They discovered another twenty head on the lee side of a rocky outcrop. Luke seemed to relax a little, joking with Glen as they worked.

In an open, windblown area they came across two frozen carcasses, a mother and her baby. The cold air stung Marilee's eyes as she looked at the poor, helpless creatures, and she fought back tears. Luke's lips drew into a grim line.

A little later the pitiful bawling of a cow drew them to the far side of a small rise. The animal was tangled in a mess of wire, and her calf lay on the ground beside her. As Luke approached, the baby lifted fearful brown eyes.

"Be careful," he warned. Wire clippers in hand, he edged around the pair. "When I let mama go, she's going to be real skittery."

Marilee reached out for Glen's arm. "Stay back, honey."

"I'm okay, Mom."

Luke snipped one piece of wire, and the cow stood, but she wasn't free yet. Even more frightened, she kicked out with a hind leg. Her hoof clipped her calf.

The young animal leapt to its feet. He dashed away screaming, which made his mother even more anxious. She lowered her shoulder into Luke, knocking him off his feet. The baby went sliding awkwardly down the slope.

"I'll get the calf," Glen announced.

"No, Son, you don't have to—"

But Marilee's warning came too late. The calf had gone slipping out onto a snow-covered pond. Glen had no way of knowing that the perfectly flat expanse of snow could be a trap with icy water below, or that the unstable weather of springtime had weakened the ice.

Because the calf was lighter and or able to spread his weight over four legs, he scampered across the pond and up the far bank. Glen wasn't so lucky.

With a crack like a rifle shot, the ice gave way, and he tumbled into the water.

Marilee screamed, "Glen!" His head vanished out of sight beneath the dark water.

Luke swore and staggered to his feet. "I'll get him."

With a final snip of his wire cutters, he freed the bawling cow, then used a controlled slide to reach the edge of the pond. He beat Marilee there by less than a second.

"Get the rope from my horse," he ordered.

"But Glen—"

"Do it now, Marilee!"

Panic pounded in her chest as Luke lay belly down on the ice and began to creep out toward the spot where Glen had slipped into the water. Her baby... Glen was her whole life!

"I can't save him without your help, Marilee! Move it!"

His words released the paralysis that had gripped her. She fled back up the hill to the horse, leading him closer to the pond. To her relief, Glen's head, with its bright strawberry curls, was showing above the water.

"Is he all right?"

"Toss the looped end of the rope to me." Luke lay spread-eagle and motionless at the very edge of the gaping hole in the ice, one hand holding the back of

Glen's jacket. At any moment their combined weight could cause the thin ice to give way.

"Oh, God..." She found the loop all right, but she'd never been into lassoing calves or twirling ropes. She hadn't even been decent at throwing a softball. She'd had no talents at all, except attracting every boy in town who had an itch in his pants.

Biting her lip to stop her chin from quivering, Marilee flung the end of the rope with all her might. The coils twisted around her legs, the loop not making it much beyond her own shadow.

"Come on, sweetheart," Luke cajoled, watching over his shoulder. "It's real cold in that water. You can do it."

She tried again, this time with more success. Even so, Luke had to stretch a long way to reach the end of the rope.

With growing dread, she watched as he worked one-handed to loop the rope around Glen's shoulders. How long had her son been in the icy water? Four or five minutes? Ten? It felt like hours.

"I got him!" Luke finally shouted. "Now tie the other end on the saddle."

Hands shaking, she did as instructed. "Okay," she called.

Luke gave a firm tug on the rope and shouted "Back!" The horse moved as ordered; the line grew taut. Marilee blessed whoever had trained the horse as her son was pulled slowly—painfully slowly—up onto the treacherous ice.

It seemed like more hours passed before both Glen and Luke were back on solid ground.

Struggling to his feet, Luke hefted the boy over his shoulder in a fireman's carry. His neck muscles corded with the effort.

Glen's lips were blue, his eyes glazed. When he coughed, Marilee thought it was the most glorious sound she'd ever heard. Her son was still alive! And Luke the most heroic man she'd ever known.

Anticipating the next move, she raced to the truck. Starting the engine, she threw the heater switch on full blast. Seconds later, Luke dumped Glen onto the front seat.

"Help me get his clothes off," he ordered.

"He'll freeze."

"No. His clothes are so wet they won't let any heat into his body."

They stripped him, working awkwardly in the close confines of the cab. When the boy was naked, his skin pink with cold, Luke retrieved a blanket from behind the seat and dried him off. By now, Marilee was sweating from exertion. Only vaguely was she aware that Luke had pulled off his soggy gloves. His hands had to be nearly frozen from exposure to the icy water.

When they were all sitting down, she slammed the truck into gear and headed back to the ranch. In the rearview mirror she caught a glimpse of the chestnut trotting along behind. She'd make sure it was one animal that would never see the inside of a glue factory.

By the time they reached the ranch house, Glen was shivering violently, his teeth chattering. That was a good sign, Marilee told herself. His deathly stillness had terrified her.

"I'm c-cold, Mom. R-real . . . cold."

"I know, honey."

Luke hefted the boy out of the truck and carried him directly to the upstairs bathroom, propping him on the edge of the tub while he let the water run until it warmed up.

"Get something hot for him to drink," he ordered. "There's hot chocolate in the cupboard, but anything will do."

Marilee raced to do as instructed. When she returned, she found her son in the tub, warm water edging up his flushed body. Luke was holding him there, talking softly, while silent tears of pain ran down Glen's cheeks.

"It's okay, Son," the rancher said, occasionally flexing his own hands to restore circulation. "That burning feeling will stop soon. It means your blood is flowing again. That's good. Real good." His rough voice was so filled with caring that Marilee was hard-pressed to check her own tears.

They got two cups of steamy hot chocolate into Glen before he began complaining, "Geez, Mom, I don't have any clothes on. A guy could use a little privacy."

"Trust me, honey. You don't have anything I haven't seen before." She smiled at him and ruffled his damp hair, her heart nearly filling her throat.

They had him soak in a second tub of hot water when the first had cooled off. Finally, Luke took his temperature and announced it had crept above ninety-eight degrees.

"Dry him off good," he suggested, handing Marilee a towel, "and bundle him up. I'll start a fire in the fireplace downstairs and he can rest on the couch. I've got to go out to check on the stock."

Marilee shot him a panicky look. "You're not going back on the range by yourself!"

The corner of his mouth turned up in a half smile. "Just to the barn. Those mama cows will have to make it on their own for the rest of the day."

Marilee knew he was counting on every calf that dropped this spring, but she was relieved he planned to stay close to home for now. Maybe by tomorrow the weather would moderate.

She offered Glen soup for lunch, which he refused. She had no appetite either. When he drifted off into a weary sleep, she put on her jacket and wandered outside. The afternoon sun cast blue shadows across the glistening white snow. So beautiful. So potentially dangerous.

She found Luke in the barn, grooming the chestnut.

"There were a couple of apples in the refrigerator," she said. "I thought maybe the horse would like a treat. My way of saying thanks."

"He did a good job, didn't he?" Luke pulled a wire brush along the animal's flank.

Marilee extended a quartered apple on her open palm. The horse nuzzled it, then delicately mouthed a single piece. "There's no way I can properly thank you, Luke. You saved my son's life."

"I did what had to be done. If he hadn't been trying to help me, he wouldn't have gotten into trouble."

As she watched Luke groom the horse, she was struck by the strength of his hands, their gentleness. Something inside her stirred—a feeling she'd repressed for a very long time.

"For what it's worth, I don't believe a man who would risk his own neck for a boy he hardly knows could be a murderer."

Resting his arm on the chestnut's rump, Luke acknowledged Marilee's statement with a simple nod of his head. His throat thickened with emotion. She couldn't know how much it meant to him to have at least one person believe him innocent. To not even think he had the capacity for that kind of a crime.

"Do you want to tell me about it?" she asked. The gelding took another piece of apple from her hand, munching softly. The whole time, Marilee's gaze locked with Luke's. In the shadowy light of the barn, her eyes looked deep green, like spring grass on the prairie.

"I was charged with hit-and-run vehicular manslaughter. One night—a lifetime ago for me—a fifteen-year-old girl was walking home along a country road when she was struck by a car and killed. The driver didn't even bother to slow down, but somebody caught the license-plate number. No one believed I wasn't the driver."

"Was it your car?"

"Nope. I was working at Jake's Garage in Newellton then. The car had been in the shop for a carburetor overhaul and oil change. The owner hadn't come to pick it up by the end of the day, so I locked it up, put the keys in Jake's office and went home. I figured the guy would stop by in the morning.''

"Maybe the owner was the driver who hit the girl. He could have had an extra key.''

"That's what I thought at the time. Except the man was out of town on business. He didn't get back until the following evening.''

"Someone else in the family could have taken the car.''

He shook his head. "He was an old guy. Divorced.''

"Could the witnesses have gotten the wrong license-plate number?''

"The next morning the car was back in Jake's lot, right where I had left it, except then the right front fender had a big dent in it." It had made Luke sick to think about the violence of the collision. More than once he had imagined the thud of flesh against metal, the young girl's scream, if she'd seen the car coming. The sounds had been almost as real as if he had been behind the wheel that night. He swallowed back the bile that was a part of his recurring nightmare.

"The forensics people found fibers from the girl's clothes on the car and matching paint chips on her body. Meanwhile, my fingerprints were all over the vehicle. The door handles and the inside had been wiped clean.''

"Wiped clean? Why would you do a thing like that?'' Marilee planted her fist on her hip. "You'd been working on the car, hadn't you? There would have been a perfectly good reason for your prints to be inside. It would have been a dumb mistake for you to try to get rid of something so obvious. Sometimes the police can be really stupid."

He grinned a little at her righteous indignation. He'd felt the same way when he was first accused. Then he'd begun to realize how very serious the cops were about nailing him for the girl's death.

Remembering, he absently combed the gelding's mane, stroking it in almost the same way he'd like to be stroking Marilee's vibrant hair. "I didn't have an alibi."

"Where were you?"

"Right here at the ranch. My dad should have been able to tell them that, but he'd been in town drinking himself into his usual nightly stupor. He got home about midnight and passed out on the couch. By the next morning, he couldn't even remember where he'd been. Everybody else knew he'd gotten soused."

"Lots of people don't have alibis on any given night. That shouldn't mean—"

"I was twenty, Marilee, and I'd sowed a lot of wild oats by that time. I was the guy on a motorcycle who terrorized old ladies and little girls, or at least that's how the good people of Newellton saw me. The original Montana bad boy with an alcoholic father, a kid who was very likely to turn out the same as his no-account old man. They figured it was better to get me off the streets as soon as possible. To protect their women and children, I suppose. A fine old Western tradition. I was just lucky hanging was out of fashion."

"But the guilty person went free."

"Yeah. I noticed." He wished there'd been a woman back then with eyes sparking in defiance, as Marilee's were—with the determined set of her delicate jaw, the absolute confidence they'd picked up the wrong guy. Maybe it would have made a difference to the cops if someone had given a damn. Maybe they'd have looked just a little further for the right guy.

His gaze settled on Marilee's lips. The lower one was slightly full, naturally sensuous. He'd wanted to bed her since the first moment she'd entered his house. But for now, he'd settle for a kiss. One kiss. It had been so damn long.

Chapter Three

Marilee saw it coming. Even so, it took her by surprise—the narrowing of his heavy-lidded gaze. The dip of his head. The light brush of his fingertips on her cheek, requesting permission.

She knew, in the instant she'd been given, that she could stop him. A simple no would work. Or the stiffening of her body. He wouldn't force her; she was sure of that. She could even back away.

Perversely—foolishly, perhaps—she didn't want him to stop. She wasn't trying to use a friendly kiss to thank him for saving her son. It was something far more personal, more needy, that welled up inside her.

She wanted to taste him, to know what his lips felt like on hers. After years of being so careful, of never letting go, she wanted to be just a little foolish.

So she let it happen.

Pleasure trembled through her at the first touch of his lips. They were warm and gentle, firm and pliable all at the same time. And strangely familiar, as though she'd been waiting all of her life for this one special kiss.

An achy weakness invaded her limbs. Behind her eyelids, unshed tears stung at the sheer hedonistic delight of his caress. She'd never known a man's fingers could be so hot, scorching her cheek with sweet tenderness right at the angle of her jaw. His scent of leather and spice and pure masculinity invaded her senses. Arousing. Tempting.

When his tongue grazed the sensitive inner surface of her lip, she felt a hot shiver of need. The reality of that feeling, all that potent desire so close to the surface, shot through her, along with all the memories she'd tried to repress.

Her hands palmed his chest. Although every one of her instincts cried out to draw this man toward her, to curl her fingers into his shirt, to link her arms around his neck, she fought the urge. She didn't dare get involved with a man who had a worse reputation than she did. What would her sister think? And the good people of Newellton? Old Myrtle Symington at the general store would have a field day, claiming the town Jezebel and the original Montana bad boy were a perfect match for each other. Marilee couldn't handle the thought of her son hearing talk like that.

Slowly, with a lingering reluctance that was echoed deep in Marilee's soul, Luke broke the kiss.

"I don't think this is a good idea." Her whispered declaration carried little conviction.

"You give me a lot of ideas." His hooded gaze swept over her face. One corner of his mouth hitched into a suggestive grin. "Most of 'em bad."

She swallowed hard, ordered her knees not to give way. "That's probably because you've been out of circulation for a while. I'm handy...." The boys in high school who'd been sowing their wild oats had thought of Marilee as a little *too* handy. Luke wasn't likely to be any different.

With lowering brows, and a voice that matched, he said, "You mean because I've been in prison for eight years, you figure I'm going to jump the first female who comes along?"

Heat scorched her cheeks. "I didn't mean that, exactly."

"Then you must mean hanging around with an ex-con isn't your idea of a good time. And you're right, Marilee. I don't have anything to offer a woman except acres of grief." A muscle was ticking in his jaw as Luke turned back to the chestnut to resume grooming. "I heard the plow go by awhile ago. When I finish here, I'll haul your car out of the ditch. Then you won't have to worry about me contaminating you or your son."

Luke's total and complete withdrawal, the absolute shuttering of all emotion, made Marilee feel like she'd been slapped. Or more accurately, as if she had slapped him. He couldn't know how much she feared the consequences of letting down her guard, even a little. She'd paid such a high price for her youthful folly. She never wanted to make the same mistake again.

In nearly fourteen years, Luke was the first man who made her question the wisdom of the vow she'd made to herself so long ago. And that scared her almost as much as seeing her son fall into the frigid pond had.

A painful band tightened around her chest. "I'll go pack up our things. Glen ought to wake up soon. I'll let you know when we're ready to leave."

Luke didn't respond. Expressionless, he kept on brushing the horse in steady strokes, not giving away any of his emotions.

Marilee wondered if that's how a man survived in prison. She was honest enough to admit that, except when it came to her son, keeping her own feelings hidden was a technique she'd honed to a fine art.

Luke secured the towing cable to the back of his pickup, then made his way through the accumulated snow to the bumper of Marilee's car. Lying on his back, he stretched to reach the axle.

He'd been stupid, that's what. To imagine he'd be satisfied with only one kiss from Marilee Haggerty was a damn fool thing to even consider. He must have been chewing on locoweed. He wanted that woman in the worst way. And it would have been the same if he had a string of women standing in line from his front porch clear into the next county.

All the kiss had done was make it abundantly clear how little he had to offer a woman.

He nicked his thumb on something sharp and swore. The sooner he could get the car out of the ditch, the sooner he could get on with his life. Alone.

In some new place, with a new job, and the past behind him.

He muscled his way out from under the vehicle. "Put the car in neutral and be sure the brake is off," he ordered as he stomped back to his truck. He didn't even look to see if Marilee had done as he'd told her. There was something so damn vulnerable in her eyes. Or maybe it was pity. At any rate, he didn't want to look at her. He didn't want to think of what might have been. He didn't want to consider Glen, either, a neat kid who would be a whole lot better off if he didn't hang around with ex-cons.

He slammed the truck into low gear and eased down on the accelerator. The truck edged forward until the cable went taut. He felt the horses under the hood straining against the weight of the car and the mound of snow that blocked its path out of the ditch. He'd shoveled the worst of it away. But maybe not enough.

He pumped on the gas. Just a little. The car broke loose from the ice and lumbered onto the dry pavement behind the truck. Luke put on the brakes.

Piece of cake.

Pleased that things had gone so well, he hopped out of the truck, intending to unhook the cable. It was then he saw the black puddle of frozen oil in the ditch. A big puddle that could only mean one thing.

With a curse, he pounded his fist on the hood of the car.

"What's wrong?" Marilee asked, getting out of the vehicle.

"Looks like when you slid off the road, you hit a rock that punched a hole in your oil pan."

"Is that bad?"

He rolled his eyes. "It means if you so much as crank over the engine, everything in there is going to seize."

"It's okay, Mom. Luke can tow us into town. There's gotta be a garage or someplace that can fix an oil pan. It can't be all that expensive."

Marilee shot her son a quelling look, but he didn't get the message. Luke was furious with her. Clearly he had no interest in taking them into town, or anywhere else. After what she'd done, after she'd hurt him so badly, Luke didn't want anything more to do with her. She couldn't really blame him.

"Get back in the car," he ordered. "And watch my brake lights. If you smash into me, the truck bumper will turn your grill to confetti."

From the gruff sound of Luke's instructions, Marilee had the distinct impression he expected her to snap to attention and salute him. *Not in this life,* she thought grimly.

"You have to send to where?" Marilee asked incredulously. She'd forgotten that small towns didn't stock every part.

"Denver. That there is where the parts depot is. Should only take a couple of days to get the oil pan here."

Marilee stood under the hoist at Jake Martins's garage, staring at the jagged hole in her oil pan. Remembering him from when she'd lived in Newellton, she guessed Jake was probably in his seventies by now. Wrinkled and whipcord lean, he still had hands perpetually stained with grease. He'd seemed a bit nervous when Luke had towed in her car. Now Jake studiously avoided meeting the younger man's eyes.

"I'll drive you on to your sister's house, if you'd like," Luke said.

She glanced around the busy garage, where three other repair bays were occupied by cars in various stages of disassembly. Evidently radio reception was better here than at Luke's ranch, because Glen had his "ears" on again and was bopping in time with the music. He seemed to be suffering no ill effects from his frigid dip in the pond.

Odd how the whole town of Newellton was so unchanged. The cars in the shop might be a few years newer than when Marilee had last been here, but the beauty shop was still next door, and Myrtle Symington's grocery store was still across the street. In the next block, Marilee had seen the store her father had owned. The sign still read Hank's Hardware, though he'd been dead for almost twenty years.

With a tremulous sigh, she said, "I think Glen and I have imposed on you enough already. I'll call Beth. I'm sure either she or her husband will be able to come pick us up."

Hands stuffed in the pockets of his sheepskin jacket, he shrugged. "I guess that's it, then. I'll be on my way back to the ranch."

Don't go. Not yet. Her frantic inner voice startled Marilee with its pleading intensity. She tamped down the impulse to say the words aloud. "Thanks for all your help."

"No problem. Hope you have a good visit with your sister."

"Yes. I'm sure we will." The formality of their parting felt painfully awkward.

Jake wiped his hands on a dirty rag and massaged his left shoulder, effectively transferring a streak of grease to his blue overalls. "You want I should order the part?"

She blinked. What she wanted was to know she'd see Luke again. But that possibility was as unlikely as it was rash. "Yes, please, Mr. Martins. Order whatever is needed."

Luke's gaze followed Jake as the old man headed toward the office.

"This is where you were working when you were arrested, isn't it?" Marilee asked.

"Yeah. I thought Jake would at least give me some sort of a character reference during the trial. But he didn't." His gaze traveled back to meet hers, his pewter eyes haunted by past betrayals.

"I'm sorry."

The air between them vibrated with tension, as if there was an emotional towing cable linking one with the other. It was a fragile bond, one that could snap at any moment. Marilee knew she ought to turn away, break the connection, but she didn't seem to have the strength of will to sever their tenuous relationship.

Vaguely, she became aware of police sirens approaching and then the squeal of brakes.

She saw Luke start and a wariness enter his eyes as he sifted his attention to the two vehicles that had blocked the front of Jake's garage. Amber and red police lights flashed on their roofs.

"What do you suppose is going on?" Marilee asked.

Luke gave an almost imperceptible shake of his head. "I'm not sure."

A uniformed deputy sheriff carrying a nightstick got out of one car and stood guarding the entrance to the repair shop. From the other vehicle, a far more distinguished man appeared. Of Native American descent, he wore a well-tailored Western suit. His dark hair was pulled back and tied with a thong. Looking stern, he settled a Stetson squarely on his head.

"Where's the owner?" he asked one of the mechanics, gesturing toward Marilee's car.

"Sheriff Hawk?" she asked tentatively. From the descriptions she'd heard, this had to be Beth's husband—a tall, dark and handsome hunk who had, in a moment of rash desperation born of love, kidnapped her sister on an Indian pony as his way of proposing. Idly Marilee wondered why it was both she and Beth found long hair on a man particularly appealing.

He shot her an assessing look. Slowly, a smile softened his stern features. "Marilee Haggerty?" When she nodded, he said, "Damn, my wife's been worried sick about you. What happened?"

Instinctively, she reached out for Luke. To protect him from false accusations. To absorb his strength. "I got lost trying to get to Newellton, and we ended up in a snowdrift. Luke Spurwood rescued us. If he hadn't, both Glen and I would probably have frozen to death."

In a studied gaze, the sheriff took Luke's measure, then extended his hand. "I don't think we've met. I'm Sheriff Hawk. My wife and I are grateful to you, Mr. Spurwood. If I can ever return the favor..."

A woman hustled past the parked police cars. "Did you catch him, Sheriff? Did you catch that man who murdered Beth's sister?"

Marilee's jaw dropped, and she could sense Luke stiffen. "No one's been murdered—" she began, then broke off abruptly. Good Lord, it was Myrtle Symington from the grocery store, sticking her beaked nose in somebody else's business. She'd always been one to jump to totally erroneous conclusions, then pass them on as gospel. Hadn't she seen Marilee get out of the car?

"I called 911, you know," Myrtle announced proudly. "I saw the car and thought it looked strange. Hadn't seen it around town before. Then I remembered the California license plate and the kind of car you all said you'd been lookin' for."

With one finger, Hawk tipped the brim of his hat up at an angle. "That was real nice of you, Myrtle. Real alert. But it turns out—"

"Millie saw it, too, right through the front window of my store," Myrtle asserted. "So we both made up our minds. We had to call when we realized who was involved." She gave Luke a scathing look. "We can't have any murderers running around free—"

"Mrs. Symington! No one has killed me or anyone else," Marilee objected. "The only thing Luke Spurwood is guilty of is rescuing me from a snowdrift." Frantically, she looked to Hawk for help. She was furious that Mrs. Symington had jumped to such a blatantly incorrect conclusion. The old busybody!

It was then Marilee spotted a second woman scurrying across the street, this one with a huge green parrot perched on her shoulder. Marilee stifled a groan. It was Millie Russell, Grandma Claire's neighbor and best friend, the woman who had lived across the street from Marilee all those years she'd been growing up—and getting into trouble. Poor Grandma had despaired for the future more than once, stuck as she had been raising her two granddaughters and caring for her widower son, who worked long hours at his store.

And to think Marilee had hoped to get in and out of town without being spotted. Right now she just wished she had a shovel to dig herself a hole. The only redeeming grace was that Glen was still hanging around at the back of the garage, oblivious to all the activity.

Millie arrived on the scene a little out of breath. "What did you find out, dear? Has the worst happened?" She peered over the top of her half glasses at Marilee.

"Reef your sails, bucko!" the parrot squawked.

"Land sakes!" Millie's hand flew to her chest. "Is that you, Marilee?"

"I'm gonna take off," Luke said under his breath.

"No. Wait." An odd sense of panic gripped Marilee. She didn't want to be left on her own with these two busybodies, and she felt slightly ill at ease with her brother-in-law. She'd never met him before and had no idea what Beth had told him, or how he might feel about her.

"As you can see, ladies," Hawk said, "Beth's sister is just fine, and we owe that to her friend, Luke Spurwood."

Three sets of beady eyes—the parrot's included—slid accusingly in Luke's direction.

"Run for your lives! Man overboard! Man overboard!"

"Hush, Charlie."

A headache threatened at the back of Marilee's skull. If anyone should have been lynched, it was these two old women. The way they spread gossip was criminal.

Somehow Hawk corralled the nosy duo and sent them back to the grocery store. Relative calm returned to Jake's Garage.

"If you've finished your business here," Hawk said, "I'll take you on home to Beth. She's been pacing the floor for two days."

"I'm sorry. Luke's phone was out of order."

Hawk nodded and glanced toward the back of the garage. "That your boy?"

"He generally prefers listening to rock music rather than talking with real people," she admitted wryly, realizing that hadn't been the case between Glen and Luke. They had truly enjoyed each other's company. Lots of guy talk, she recalled.

"Well, let's get going then. I'll call Beth from the car to let her know you're both okay."

She glanced up at Luke. With hooded eyes, he was staring at the sheriff.

Rarely did Marilee do anything impulsively. At least, she hadn't since she'd left Newellton. And she certainly didn't know her brother-in-law well enough to involve him in somebody else's business. But he was the county sheriff. And Myrtle's assumption that Luke's conviction of manslaughter made him a suspect in any other case still galled Marilee. It was so darn unfair....

"Hawk, Luke has recently been released from prison."

"I know that. The word's been out for a while that he moved back to the ranch on the old county road."

"Not much stays a secret around here, does it?" Luke commented.

"Not much," Hawk agreed.

"Planning to keep an eye on me?"

"I like to keep close tabs on all my constituents."

Marilee didn't like the way the two men were sparring with each other. "Luke's innocent, Hawk. He wants a chance to prove he never should have been sent to jail."

Hawk's eyebrows drew into a skeptical frown.

"It's true," she persisted. "You said if he needed a favor, all he had to do is ask. You're in a position to help him clear his name."

Raising his eyes, Hawk looked straight at Luke, his gaze probing. "How do you feel about that?"

When Luke didn't immediately respond, the silence dragged on, broken only by the sound of a power wrench somewhere in the garage and someone else slamming a trunk lid.

Marilee held her breath. Maybe he wasn't innocent at all. Maybe it had been all blustery talk and wishful thinking on Luke's part that he wanted to clear his name. Maybe she should have kept her mouth shut.

Maybe, once again, she'd foolishly misjudged a man.

Chapter Four

Luke jammed his fists back into his jacket pockets.

He didn't like accepting favors from a cop.

Worse, he knew he ought to stay as far away as
possible from Marilee Haggerty. To a man who hadn't
experienced any compassion in the last eight years,
and not a hell of a lot before that, she was a little too
caring. At her core she was soft, and he had learned
how to deal with hard. Hanging around with a woman
like Marilee, a man could get himself into serious
trouble thinking about things that weren't likely to
happen.

But in his gut he wanted the holier-than-thou folks
of Newellton to know he hadn't been the one to kill
that teenage girl. To do that, he needed Hawk.

"I could use your help," he admitted cautiously.

The sheriff nodded. "Why don't you drop by the house after supper? We'll talk then. Right now I've got to get Marilee home or my wife will have paced a path right through the flooring of the living room."

"I'll be there."

"You know where my place is? North of town?"

"I've been past a time or two." Only a year or so old, the sheriff's house nestled between a low bluff and a creek lined with cottonwoods. Luke had envied a family that could afford that kind of simple luxury.

"Hawk's right about being on our way," Marilee said, her blue-green eyes mapping Luke's face as if she thought INNOCENT ought to be stamped in capitals across his forehead. "We'd better be going before the rest of the town reports my premature demise to Beth. I'll see you this evening?"

"Sure."

"Come on, Glen." She waved to her son, trying to attract his attention, and mouthed, "We have to go." She didn't know what was causing the biggest knots of anxiety in her stomach—Luke's apparent reluctance to accept Hawk's help, the fact she was about to see her sister for the first time in fourteen years or the thought she'd be seeing Luke again that evening.

After lowering the hoist, Hawk helped her empty the car and loaded his vehicle with suitcases and the presents for Beth's baby. Luke slipped away without much of a goodbye, leaving Marilee feeling empty and unfulfilled. Then, before she could entirely gather her wits, Hawk had driven them the few miles to his house.

As soon as she got out of the car, a bad case of paralysis took hold of Marilee. Emotion tightened her throat so thickly she could hardly breathe, and her eyes stung with the threat of tears. Her feet felt as though she were wearing lead-lined boots. Her little sister, now a lovely young woman, stood on the front porch with a six-month-old baby in her arms. All Marilee could think about was the desperately lonely years she had let slip by because she had been too ashamed to come home.

"Hey, Mom, are you going all weird or somethin'?" Glen stared at her as if she'd gone terminally dumb.

Her son's typically adolescent comment—and his too-accurate assessment—unlocked Marilee's paralysis. The tears sprang to the surface. Freed from the immobility of the past, she ran toward the porch. Beth met her halfway. They hugged and cried and laughed, rocking together with each sobbing breath.

"I'm so glad you came—"

"You look wonderful—"

"I missed you so much—"

"I'm sorry—"

"It's all right—"

"You're all grown up—"

Their breathless words tumbled on top of each other, as if in the first few seconds of being together again after so many years they could make up for what they had missed.

The squirming child in Beth's arms finally fussed enough to interrupt the reunion.

"Oh, let me see little Sarah," Marilee pleaded, wiping her eyes with the back of her hand. The baby hid her face in Beth's neck, but not before Marilee got a good look at saucer-size brown eyes and a little, turned-up nose. "Adorable."

Hawk spoke up. "I thought we did pretty good for a first effort." Pride shone in his dark eyes.

"First?" Beth asked. Her hair was more blond than strawberry, with a thousand vibrant ringlets that danced as she tossed her head. "Are you suggesting there's going to be a second?"

His lips lifted in a teasing grin. "Whenever you're ready, sweetheart, you know I'm willing to do my part."

A flush swept up Beth's face. "You're impossible," she said with a groan. She reached out to include Glen in the family circle. "You're not too big to hug, are you?"

"Naw, I guess not." His cheeks turned the same fiery red as Beth's, an affliction common to all the Haggertys.

Marilee was struck by how much her son had missed by not being part of a larger family. She'd done that to him. There'd been no aunts and uncles to dote on him or give him extra hugs. Most of all, he hadn't had a father to glow with pride at his smallest accomplishment.

The image of Luke popped into her mind—the way he and Glen had shared an easy masculine bond. And the way he had kissed her.

She shook the mental picture away. Neither she nor her son needed an added complication in their lives.

Establishing a new home and getting reacquainted with the family she already had would be enough for now. Still, a small part of her reckless heart, a piece she thought sure she'd excised over the years, looked forward to seeing Luke again.

She hadn't meant to be lying in wait for him in the living room. She'd been sent in search of Sarah's straying teddy bear, which Beth suspected had been dropped sometime before dinner. But there Luke was, coming out of Hawk's office after their meeting, and Marilee had a hard time repressing the surge of pleasure that rippled through her. He was wearing a pair of new jeans that clung to his lean hips and a cable-knit sweater in dark blue that seemed to emphasize the breadth of his shoulders. He'd shaved recently, and it looked like he'd had his hair trimmed, though it was still long enough to tempt a woman to explore the rich, thick strands.

Self-consciously, she hugged the well-loved stuffed animal to her chest. "How'd it go?"

"Okay, I guess." He looked uncomfortable, as though he wanted to hightail it out of there but didn't want to appear rude. "Hawk's going to get me a copy of the trial transcript."

"You think that will help?"

"I don't know. As I remember, most of the testimony was technical stuff. Blood, fingerprints, dented fenders—that sort of thing."

"Sounds like pretty dull reading." If he wanted to leave, she wouldn't stop him. He was a free man, after all.

"Hawk thought I ought to try to talk with everyone who had a key to Jake's office. Everyone who had access to Rutherford's car keys that night."

"Is that going to be a big job?"

"Probably not. A half-dozen people, at most. I assume somebody talked to them before, but my public defender wasn't worth much. Hawk's going to check the records." His gaze slid from her to the large oil painting over the fireplace, a portrait of a reclining nude woman with only a slender drape of cloth covering her most private parts. "When did you pose for that?"

Marilee flushed a hundred shades of crimson. "That's not me! It's our Grandma Claire. Some artist passed through Newellton in the thirties doing portraits for room and board, and whatever cash he could earn. Beth found that picture in the attic of the old house when she was cleaning it out after Grandma died. It's supposed to be worth a lot of money now. Museum quality, they say."

"It must have caused some talk for a woman to pose nude back in the thirties."

"No one knew at the time, though Beth found out there had been some gossip about Grandma Claire and the artist. That's probably why she was always telling Beth and me to be careful of our reputations." Wisdom that Marilee had totally ignored as a teenager. The repeated warnings had made her even more ashamed to let her grandmother know where she'd run off to, or about the baby she was raising on her own.

Cocking his head to one side, he studied the painting more closely. "You and your grandmother could have been twins."

"Oh, go on...." The heat in her cheeks rose another several degrees. She didn't compare to the surprising beauty her grandmother had been as a young woman.

"I'm serious. You've got the same eyes, the same kind of pouty lower lip. Your figure is just as full and lush. And your hair..." He turned toward Marilee, his gaze narrowing on her. "I'd like to see you wear your hair down around your shoulders like that. You'd be sensational."

Totally nonplussed, she fingered the neat coil at her nape, a style she had intentionally adopted to ward off unwanted advances. Obviously her ploy hadn't worked with Luke. "Sometimes a woman isn't comfortable having men think of her as...sensational."

"Why not?" He looked genuinely puzzled.

"Because they somehow think if a woman is attractive, she's also..." she searched for a word that wouldn't sound too crass "...*available*."

He lifted a lean hip and settled it on the back of one of the Western-style love seats flanking the fireplace. "You don't want men to think you're beautiful?"

"Not really."

"It's created some problems for you?"

"A few," she conceded, uncomfortable with his probing questions.

"Are we talking about Glen's father here?"

She shrugged noncommittally. "Among others."

"Let me make a wild guess." He folded his arms across his chest. "You said you once ran away and found your troubles had gone along with you. I'd say you ran away from Newellton because you were pregnant with Glen. You couldn't have been much older than a kid yourself."

"Old enough that I should have known better. I was seventeen."

"I gather the guy involved wasn't interested in taking responsibility for what had happened."

She lifted her chin a degree or two. There were no secrets in Newellton. At least not for long. And she'd told Glen the truth since the beginning—as much as he'd needed to know—that she and his father had been young and foolish, and maybe a little bit in love, but not nearly mature enough to handle the responsibilities that went with a long-term relationship. Other details she'd omitted—like the condemning attitude of Bud's parents. She'd never wanted her son to feel the sting of their rejection. "I'm sure half the town would be happy to confirm your conclusions, at least about me running away because I was pregnant. My relationship with Glen's father was no secret."

He nodded thoughtfully. "And that's why you were so quick to defend me at Jake's Garage? Because you hate those old biddies in town and how they talked about you years ago?"

"Myrtle Symington wasn't exactly kind to me when I was a teenager." Normally not a vindictive person, Marilee had over the years conjured up a thousand different appropriate punishments for the nosiest woman in town. They ranged from pins stuck in a voodoo doll to locking her in a room filled with deaf people.

"So where's Glen's father now?"

Making a big to-do about straightening a cushion, she said, "Look, I wouldn't have even considered coming back to this town, or even coming back to Montana, if Glen's father was still in the picture. A few months ago Beth mentioned he'd been killed in a car accident. His widow and their children moved back to Seattle, where her family lives." There were other relatives in Newellton, though, she realized. Bud's parents were still prominent local residents and Marilee hoped to avoid them.

Luke shoved away from the couch and came to stand closer to Marilee. Too close, she thought, her heart thrumming an erratic beat against her rib cage. He was so near she caught the spicy scent of his aftershave.

"I wasn't being critical of you, so you don't have to go all bristly. Remember me? I'm the original bad boy. I'm not about to throw stones at you for something that happened a long time ago, when every window in my glass house has already been pretty well shattered."

That took the steam out of her defensive posture. "I'm sorry."

"You do look a lot like your grandmother." He'd softened his tone to a rough caress.

"Thank you."

"I didn't mean to upset you."

"It's okay. I'm probably a little sensitive on the subject."

He grinned. "Both you and your grandmother are sexy as hell."

"Luke, will you cut that out!" Marilee turned away, but she knew he'd seen the quick blush rise to her cheeks. For years she'd kept her emotions in check. Now this gray-eyed devil was making her forget everything she'd struggled so hard to learn.

MTV was playing in the other room; Glen was gorging himself after his brief hiatus from hard-rock music. Upstairs, Beth was cooing to Sarah as she bathed her and Hawk was still in his office. Marilee felt strangely alone and vulnerable, defenseless against Luke's powerful virility. She wanted to run—clear back to L.A. if she had to—instead of suffering through the torment of this achy feeling she got whenever he was around.

She felt the light brush of his fingertips at the back of her neck, no more than the teasing of a few strands of loose hair at her nape. Warmth stole through her and curled into her midsection. He shouldn't touch her like that. Not so gently that it made her forget the consequences of giving in to impulses that were better kept in check.

"Hawk also said I ought to take a witness along when I interview the people who had access to the car keys that night." The husky timbre of his voice rasped along nerve endings Marilee had forgotten existed. "That way they can't tell me one thing and the cops something else."

"That makes sense." What didn't make sense was how she imagined she could feel Luke's warm breath on her neck. Or how much she wished he would kiss her at the sensitive juncture of her neck and shoulder.

"I don't know many people in Newellton anymore and even fewer I would trust."

Her knees felt extraordinarily weak. She wanted to lean back into Luke's strength. And didn't dare do that. "That presents a problem."

"Would you come along?"

Say no, an inner voice warned. It would simply add grist for the town gossips for her to be seen with Luke, a man they all believed to be a felon. It would be like waving a red flag in their faces. *See, Marilee Haggerty is still as wild as she ever was. She hasn't changed a bit.*

But it was blatantly unfair that the townspeople judged both her and Luke so harshly. Someone ought to have the courage to shake them out of their ivory towers.

"I'm not sure how much help I'd be," she hedged. "And I want to spend lots of time with Beth and the baby."

"How about you give it a try? If it gets too complicated, or if things don't work out, no harm done."

That was true. Marilee had no intention of staying in Newellton long. In the eyes of the townspeople, she could hardly make her reputation any worse, and what they thought of her was unimportant anyway. Or so she had told herself time and again, with little success.

She turned and looked up into a pair of gray eyes so dark and filled with sexual hunger they nearly took her breath away. With difficulty, she tamped down the matching desire that threatened to overwhelm her. Swallowing hard, she asked, "When do we start?"

"Tomorrow."

"How in tarnation am I supposed to remember a thing like that?" Jake Martins stuck his head back under the hood of the car he'd been working on.

"My arrest was the biggest thing that had happened in Newellton for years. The police must have questioned you. People don't forget a thing like that. All I'm asking is who else could have gotten into the office and taken Rutherford's car keys?"

Jake moved around to the opposite side of the engine compartment. "You accusin' me of killin' that girl?"

"Mr. Martins, we're not accusing anyone," Marilee insisted. "Luke is simply trying to prove he wasn't the one driving Rutherford's car that night."

"Seems a might late to be worrying about that, don't it? You already been in jail. No sense to open that can o' worms agin."

Luke speared his fingers through his hair. He'd never understood why Jake had turned so cold toward him. When he'd first started working for him, the old man had been like a teacher, maybe even the father he wished he'd had. In return, Luke had eagerly soaked up every bit of knowledge he could about engines and power drives and all the mechanical idiosyncracies that made up the world of auto mechanics. He'd always felt more at home with a wrench in his hand than with a pair of reins or a pitchfork. Jake had encouraged his dream of owning his own repair shop one day. Then the world had crashed in on Luke with his arrest, and Jake hadn't seemed to give a damn.

"I remember there was a mechanic named Pete something," Luke now said. "Is he still around?"

"Pete Williams. Moved to Missouri a few years back."

Luke made a note of the name, but doubted it would do him much good. "What about that older guy? Everybody called him Curly."

"Ain't my job to keep track of every Tom, Dick and Harry who works here. Curly left. That's all I know. And I wouldn't have given either him or Pete the keys to the office. They would'a ripped me off, the both of 'em."

"But you gave *me* the keys, Jake. Dammit, you trusted me." Luke's anger rose a notch. What the hell had made Jake turn against him?

Marilee touched his arm. Though the weather had warmed considerably, she wore a soft, clingy sweater, the kind a man ached to caress with his hands.

"This isn't going to do you any good," she said.

She might be right, but Luke had spent too many hours dreaming about clearing his name to give up so easily. "What about that woman who did the paperwork?" he persisted, remembering a narrow-faced woman who came in a couple of times a week to pick up the work orders and handle the payroll. "What was her name?"

"Arletta Finch, and she still does my books for me. But she sure ain't no criminal. Got herself a flock of grandkids now."

"I remember her," Marilee said. "She had a daughter who was in my class at Newellton High. I doubt that Arletta is much of a suspect."

"I suppose not." Luke searched his brain for someone else, anyone who might have gotten into the office that night. "How about your grandson? Seems to me Andy used to help out around here. Did he have a key?"

Jake mumbled something from under the hood.

"What?"

The mechanic stood and rubbed a muscle in his shoulder. "I said, this ain't got nothin' to do with my grandson. He was a good boy. Besides, he moved away years ago, so you cain't go blaming nothin' on him."

"Where'd he go?"

"Cain't say as how I'd tell you even if I knew." He lowered the hood, pressing down until the latch caught. "I got work to do and no time to answer any more of your fool questions."

As Jake turned his back and walked away, Luke felt a knot of tension tighten in his gut. He hadn't learned a damn thing that was useful. No wonder Hawk had been skeptical about reopening the investigation after so many years.

"He's lying."

Luke gave Marilee a puzzled look. "You think Jake was the one driving the hit-and-run car?"

She shrugged. "I just know he never once looked you in the eye, and he didn't yesterday, either, when we brought in my car for repair. My intuition tells me the man is trying to hide something."

"Maybe he feels guilty that he didn't stand up for me after I was arrested."

"Maybe."

In a gesture so natural Luke wondered why he hadn't done it before, he looped his arm around Marilee's shoulders. "Let's go find Arletta. Maybe her memory is better than Jake's."

"Beth asked me to stop at the grocery store for milk. She's already figured out teenage boys have hollow legs." She slid out from under his arm, leaving him holding air and wishing for more. Damn, she felt good. Smelled good, too. Sultry and sexy. She was more woman than most men could handle, though he wasn't sure she'd be willing to admit that. Maybe she didn't even know.

"What's Glen doing today?" he asked as they headed across the street, the two of them separated now by the few feet of space she'd put between them. The high color in her cheeks suggested she wasn't as immune to his touch as she might want to let on. But then, maybe she was a lot smarter than him, knowing there wasn't a chance in Hades the two of them could get together.

"He went to the county seat with Hawk this morning. The lure of a computer that could tap into half the world's criminal archives was too much for him to resist."

Luke chuckled. "At least he'll take off his ears for a while."

"Don't count on it. He took them along in case he got bored. I'm not sure even total mayhem would make him give up his music for long."

"I used to be that way about anything with an engine in it."

Pausing at the entrance to the grocery store, she glanced up at him. "That's why you worked at Jake's Garage?"

"Yeah. I had this idea I'd own my own shop someday. I still plan to if I can sell the ranch and clear enough to set up somewhere."

"I hope it works out for you."

Marilee shoved through the door to the grocery store, knowing full well dreams didn't always come true. As an adolescent, she'd had visions of happily-ever-afters. But no sooner had she told Bud Franklin he was going to be a father than he was gone. Vanished. And his father wouldn't tell her where he was, or when he'd come back, accusing her of lying about his son being the one who had gotten her pregnant. She'd always wondered if Taylor Franklin had spread even more rumors about her, but couldn't imagine why he'd bother.

Bud, who had apparently outdistanced both the U.S. Postal Service and AT&T, never once made an effort to contact her.

So she'd left town. It had probably been impulsive, and undoubtedly stupid, but she hadn't wanted Grandma Claire to know about her shame. There had already been enough talk about Marilee Haggerty. For once, she'd even been relieved both of her parents were deceased.

Fourteen years ago she'd learned two important lessons she didn't dare forget at this late date: she didn't belong in Newellton and men had an unpleasant tendency to abandon her.

She picked out a gallon of milk from the refrigerator case. "I think I'll get some frozen burritos for Glen," she told Luke. "They're good for stuffing hollow legs."

"He's a lucky kid to have a mother who worries about him so much."

"It goes with the territory, and I don't mind. He's the best thing that ever happened to me." She'd learned to count the blessings she had, not dream about those she might want.

They had the grocery store almost to themselves, so when Marilee placed her selections on the checkout counter, Myrtle Symington was in no hurry to ring up the bill.

Luke casually thumbed through a magazine. "Say, Myrtle, do you remember that guy named Curly who used to work over at Jake's?"

"He's got mechanics that come 'n go faster than flies being chased by a swatter." She punched the price of milk into the cash register. "None of my business when a man like Curly takes up with some fast woman over Harlowton way. If he wants to pair up with some gal who's already got a couple of kids, that's fine with me."

Nodding encouragingly, Luke said, "How 'bout Jake's grandson? I thought Andy might end up owning the garage. He used to hang around a lot."

Myrtle's fingers hovered above the register keys. "That boy was odd. Really odd. He liked to mix cherry cola with root beer. Enough to make you sick, isn't it?''

Marilee tended to agree.

"He left town six, seven years ago, if memory serves,'' Myrtle continued. "Don't know why, except him and Jake hadn't been getting along real good for a while. Arguing and shouting across the street there, like nobody could hear 'em. I always say a body ought to keep his fights indoors, where they won't bother nobody else.''

"What were they fighting about?'' Luke asked.

"Weren't none of my business.'' She rang up the burritos and put the order in a paper sack. "I was just plain glad the boy left before he and his grandpa came to blows.''

Hefting the bag of groceries, Luke wondered why a man and his grandson would suddenly start fighting when previously they'd been pretty tight. It could have been normal adolescent rebellion, he supposed. But the timing was damn coincidental.

In a town the size of Newellton, someone ought to have the answers. Arletta Finch was as good a bet as any.

Chapter Five

"All I know about are which bills to pay and which to hold off on, deposits for the bank and the payroll. Jake doesn't hire me to stick my nose in his personal business."

A converted front porch served as Arletta Finch's office. Neat stacks of folders covered a worktable, and filing cabinets filled the rest of the crowded space. The woman hadn't been eager to talk with Luke and Marilee and wasn't being receptive to their questions now. Marilee wondered why.

"We thought maybe you'd know why Jake and Andy argued so much."

Narrow faced and harried, the bookkeeper glanced from Marilee to Luke and back again. "Look, once a week I go to the garage to pick up the invoices from vendors and the time cards. The next day, I take in the paychecks. I've got no time to hang around for social visits."

"Do you know if Andy had a key to the office?" Luke asked.

She raised her narrow shoulders in a helpless shrug. "I can't tell you anything. I just can't. My job..."

From somewhere inside the house came a thumping sound and a shouted, "Arly!"

Arletta reacted with a quick turn of her head. "That's Jed, my husband. He bangs his cane when he doesn't think he can shout loud enough to be heard, which isn't often the case. Arthritis has got him so bad he hasn't been able to get around good in years. I've got to go see to him."

"If you think of anything, anything at all," Luke said, "would you let me or Marilee know? Please."

"I remember you were a bit of a wild one, Luke, but seems to me you never missed a day of work." A flicker of regret appeared in her eyes, then just as quickly vanished. "I'm sorry." Turning, she went into the main house, leaving them to let themselves out on their own.

As Marilee reached Luke's truck, she said, "Arletta knows something. I'm sure she does."

"She was evasive," Luke conceded, opening the door for Marilee. "Maybe she just doesn't want to get involved. It looks to me like she needs the money she gets for taking care of Jake's books."

Another dead end, Marilee thought as she climbed into the truck.

It had been three days since they'd gotten the feeling Jake or his grandson were somehow involved in the hit-and-run for which Luke had been convicted. It had taken that long before Jake's bookkeeper had agreed to see them. Marilee was convinced someone in Newellton knew what had really happened.

But no one was talking. Not Myrtle Symington and not Arletta Finch. Certainly not Jake Martins.

The futility of their efforts and the townspeople's apparent conspiracy of silence grated on Marilee's sense of fair play.

Luke slid into the driver's seat.

"If I were you I'd be spitting tacks by now with everybody being so damn tight-lipped about that hit-and-run," Marilee said.

One side of his mouth lifted in a half grin. "You're cute when you get mad."

She grimaced. "You're supposed to be clearing your name, not worrying about how I look. Don't you ever lose your temper?"

"Not often. Not anymore." Starting the engine, he pulled away from the curb and headed back toward Hawk's house. "You learn pretty quick in prison to keep your thoughts to yourself. Getting angry does nothing but get you in trouble, either with the guards or the other cons."

His sobering admission brought Marilee up short. "Was it awful to be in jail?"

"Not exactly a walk in the park." Turning onto the main road north of town, Luke remembered the worst part had been the terrible sense the world was passing him by, that through no fault of his own he was wasting the best years of his life.

And nobody gave a damn. His dad had come to see him maybe twice in the early years, using the excuse that he couldn't come more often because it was a long way from home and he had to take care of the stock. The truth was his dad would rather have stayed home and drunk himself senseless than go a quarter mile out of his way to see his son. He only worked the ranch hard enough to keep himself well-stocked in booze.

When his unresponsive silence lengthened, Marilee asked, "You don't like to talk about it?"

"Not particularly." He didn't want to remember how he'd been forced to live on the edge of violence to avoid the cons who bullied anybody who showed so much as an instant of weakness. Remembering the feel of knuckles bruised and bloodied in more than one fight, he flexed his fingers around the steering wheel. He'd been tough enough to survive. That's all that mattered. From now on he'd toe the line, whatever it took. He was never going back inside.

Marilee nodded, studying Luke's grim expression. The taut way he clenched his jaw and the slight flare of his nostrils told of his emotional pain. She wouldn't pursue the subject. There were a lot of details in her own past she didn't want to recall.

He turned the truck into the long driveway leading to Hawk's house. Warm days had melted much of the snow dropped by the spring blizzard, leaving splotches of bare ground already tinted green with the first shoots of grass. The air was fresh with the scent of new growth.

Unobtrusively, Marilee slid Luke another glance. Was he the cause of her strange feeling of buoyancy these days, in spite of the fact they were getting few answers about the crime for which he had been convicted? Or was it simply the age-old promise of spring that made her step a little lighter?

They'd seen each other every day, though always under the guise of pursuing their amateur detective work. In spite of herself, Marilee had begun looking forward to his arrival and feeling his absence when he left. Without her realizing just how it had happened, they'd slipped into a relationship that teetered somewhere between friendship and being lovers. A dangerous game of brinkmanship for a woman who had vowed never to be vulnerable to a man again.

Luke parked, and together they went into the house. Though Marilee was only a guest and Luke a visitor, she had an odd feeling about the rightness of their walking side by side into a place that felt very much like home.

"Hello, you two," Beth called from the back of the house. "I'm in the studio."

"That means Sarah is napping," Marilee explained. "It's the only time Beth can get any work done. Or in the middle of the night, of course."

"I can believe that. For such a tiny thing, Sarah's a real firecracker."

Beth was busy at her drawing table. Across the top of the canted surface, four illustrations of Rico the Recycling Man were spread out, evidently the latest in environmentally correct characters for children's books. Beth had a true flair for seeing humor in the people she concocted, and the publisher was well pleased by how she combined vitality with the message.

"How'd it go?" she asked, without looking up.

"Arletta wasn't too talkative."

"That's too bad." Her brush formed a curved line beneath one of the figures. "Glen rode Hawk's bike into town. Said he was just going to hang out and would be back before dinner."

"He's probably going to check out the record store," Marilee said.

Beth finished putting rubbery black legs on the last aluminum can marching toward Rico's recycling bin. She swiveled around on her chair, raising her gaze to Luke. "Hawk had one of his deputies bring over the transcript of your trial. I put it on the coffee table in the living room."

"Thanks." He looked at Marilee, and she gestured with her head that he should go ahead. She knew how anxious he was to read the transcript.

When he had left the room, Beth leaned back, tapping the end of her paintbrush to her chin. "So how are you two getting along?"

"What? Me and Luke?" Marilee bluffed with a casual shrug. "We're not *getting along,* as you put it. Your husband was the one who suggested Luke have a witness when he interviews people."

"Sure. And that's why you hang around the front door when you're expecting him to show up, just like I did with Hawk. You can't fool your little sister. You're smitten with that guy. After all these years, it's none of my business, but ..." She tugged at her lower lip with her teeth, just as she had as a kid, when

Grandma Claire caught her committing some transgression.

"But what?"

"Hawk has talked with the investigating officer in Luke's case. He doesn't think there's much chance Luke will be able to prove he didn't kill that girl."

A painful knot tightened in Marilee's stomach. Her feelings for Luke must be terribly transparent to have Beth even discuss the case with her. What had happened to the protective mask she'd worn for so many years? "He has a right to try," she avowed.

"I know that, and so does Hawk. It's just that I don't want you to do anything...foolish."

"Like I did when I was seventeen?" Fall for some guy, only to be left in the lurch.

"You couldn't *save* Bud from his father back then and you can't save Luke either. Not if he's guilty."

Marilee went very still. "What do you mean?"

"I know I wasn't very old when you ran away—only eleven—and maybe I didn't understand everything that was going on, but I had the distinct impression you started dating Bud Franklin because you thought he needed you."

"His father was so hard on him. He expected Bud to be the perfect son—a star football player, a genius in class. Bud tried, but he never lived up to his father's expectations."

"And now you're falling for some other guy who needs you? A man with a prison record?"

Turning away, Marilee pressed her forearms to her midsection in the hope of holding down all the conflicting feelings that threatened to well up in her. The needs she'd denied, the loneliness she'd endured, the wanting that had suddenly resurfaced—emotions she didn't dare admit. "I know he's an ex-con," she whispered. "And I'm fully aware I have a son to think about." Plus her own very fragile heart. She knew what it was like to lack the respect of others. A man with a prison record would relearn that same lesson a thousand times over.

"I can understand you feeling that Glen needs a father."

Marilee whirled, her jaw clenched with the effort to not let go of her control. To not let even her sister see all the things she needed, too. "I can take care of my son. I've been doing it for thirteen years."

Beth paled. "I'm sorry. I didn't mean to butt in—"

"Oh, God..." Cursing her own weakness, Marilee wrapped her arms around Beth's shoulders. Since she was sitting on a stool, they were very nearly the same height. "I'm the one who's sorry. I've forgotten how to be a decent sister. Maybe I never knew."

"Of course you did. You were the best. You even let me watch you put all that gooey makeup on every morning."

"I did?"

"Well, maybe you didn't know I was watching," Beth conceded, a wry grin in her voice. "You probably didn't know I was peeking out the window when you were kissing your dates good-night on the front porch, either."

"Grandma would have had a fit."

"Now that I think of it, you probably didn't know I stole your bras and stuffed them with socks, then pranced around school."

Marilee choked down a laugh. "You didn't? In my bras?"

"I don't think I was a very convincing as a femme fatale, at least not when I was ten years old."

Torn between tears and laughter, Marilee said, "You have no idea how much I missed you, you pesky little squirt. If I'd known you were stealing my bras, I wouldn't have given you a second thought."

"I'll bet." Beth wiped the back of her hand across her tear-dampened cheek. "Look, if we get too maudlin here, I'll never get my sketches done in time to meet my deadline. I'm just glad you're home, sis."

"Me, too." Emotion tightened Marilee's throat and the sting of tears pressed at the back of her eyes.

"Be careful with Luke. He probably doesn't remember me from school—I was too young—but I remember him as being pretty wild. I don't want you to get hurt. He's the kind of guy who could tempt the socks off a girl before she knew what hit her."

"I've noticed." Marilee realized with only a few words spoken, her sister understood the emotions that were roiling unchecked through her system. Maybe Beth had fought the same sort of demons during her courtship with Hawk, she mused as she went in search of Luke.

Sitting on the couch, he was hunched over the coffee table, slowly turning the pages as he read the testimony that had sent him to prison. A lock of dark, silken hair had slipped down over his forehead. Unconsciously, he shoved it back, to no avail, and that small gesture made him look vulnerable. As though he might need someone . . . someone like her.

His wool shirt was open at the collar, allowing an enticing glimpse of curling hair above the line of his T-shirt. Marilee already knew his chest was broad and unyielding. She wondered what swirling pattern covered that solid expanse and how it would feel beneath her hands.

In another time, another place, Marilee might have found Luke an easy man to love. But fourteen years of distrust had left their mark. The supports she used to protect both herself and her son were none too steady. There were some risks she simply didn't dare take.

She bit her lower lip to halt an unwelcome quiver of regret.

As though he had heard the quick breath she'd drawn, he raised his gaze. Pewter eyes snared her in a warm trap of desire.

She swallowed hard. "Are you finding anything useful?"

"Like I told you, they found my fingerprints almost everywhere except inside the car."

"Then obviously it must have been someone else driving the car that night. You had a perfectly legitimate reason to leave prints."

"I wish you'd been my attorney. My public defender didn't manage to point out that little discrepancy. Hell, the guy only spent about thirty minutes with me before the case went to trial."

Maybe the attorney had been incompetent, or lazy. Or maybe, she thought with some dismay, Newellton's conspiracy of silence was so tightly wound there was no hope of Luke clearing his name.

The front door opened and a gust of cool air preceded Glen's arrival in the house. Without so much as a hello, he started down the hallway to the guest room.

Fear slammed into Marilee's stomach. Her son's shirttail was hanging out, the sleeve was torn and his face—

"Glen! What happened?"

"I'm okay, Mom." Instead of wearing his earphones, which connected him to the world of rock music, he had them hooked around his neck.

"Let me see you."

He hung his head and turned his face away as she approached. "It's nothin', Mom. Really."

With her fingertips, she turned his head back to her. She winced at the sight of his swollen left eye and his bruised cheek. "A fight? Here in Newellton? Why, for heaven sake? We don't even know anyone in town."

"It was just some guys, Mom. They said some things, that's all."

"About what?"

He shot Luke a glance. "Just things."

"About Luke?" she persisted.

"Partly."

Luke stood. "They told you I'd been in prison?"

"Is it true?"

"Yes."

The determined hero worship in Glen's eyes wavered, and Marilee ached at her failure to tell her son about Luke's past.

"You really killed some girl?" Glen asked.

"There was a car accident, a hit-and-run. I wasn't the guy driving, but I doubt there's anyone in Newellton besides your mother who would believe that." Luke tucked his fingers into his back pockets. "You didn't have to stick up for me, Son. I can take care of myself."

"It wasn't just you they were talking about."

Luke's eyes narrowed.

Dread tightened Marilee's chest. "What were they saying, Glen?"

He shrugged and color rose to his cheeks. "They said it figured you two would hang around together. That you were two of a kind."

The dread she'd been feeling turned to nausea, roiling through her stomach. She swallowed back the bitter taste of bile. After all these years, no one had forgotten how wild she'd been. Or forgiven her for it.

Now her son was paying for the sins of her past.

"Go ask your aunt Beth if she's got an ice bag for that eye, to stop the swelling."

"I'm sorry, Mom. I know you don't like me to fight."

Struggling against the press of tears, she gave him a quick hug. "It's not your fault."

"How bad does the other guy look?" Luke asked.

A tentative smile nearly closed Glen's swollen eye. "He was bigger than me, but I still got in a swing or two."

Luke nodded. "Good for you."

Marilee gritted her teeth until Glen was out of hearing. "Please don't encourage my son to fight."

"Sometimes that's what a man has to do."

"Not... my... son." She enunciated each word distinctly to make sure Luke got the message. "I moved him away from L.A. so he wouldn't have to battle his way through school. I don't want him fighting."

Lowering his voice, he said, "Are you really that upset about fighting in general, or are you mad about *why* he was fighting this time?"

The truth of his words battered her conscience. She didn't want to hurt Luke. Even more so, she needed to shield her son.

"I just think... Listen, this isn't working out," she said taking a deep breath. "It would be better if I spent more time with Beth and Sarah."

The pain of rejection flashed in his eyes. "I understand." He snatched up the pages of transcript from the coffee table. "Tell Sheriff Hawk I'll be in touch if I learn anything."

"I will." Her clenched fists trembled in denial of her instinctive desire to soothe his anger. Her primary responsibility—her *only* responsibility—was to her son.

Her foolish behavior had already cost Glen a black eye. She wouldn't subject him to more harassment from the good folks of Newellton. What she needed or wanted didn't matter.

Luke stopped right in front of her, so close she was forced to look up into his steel gray eyes. For an instant she saw his pain, and then the shuttered wariness returned. "Keep out of blizzards, Marilee Haggerty," he warned in a low, raspy voice. "You never know who you're going to meet."

Cold air swirled around her as Luke went out the front door, but it was the icy feeling inside that made Marilee shiver. Alone. She was so terribly alone.

She was still standing like an ice sculpture in the middle of the living room several minutes later when the doorbell rang.

Her heart leapt into her throat. *Luke!* He'd come back. He didn't hate her. He understood that she had to protect her son. It didn't mean she couldn't care about him. But here, in Newellton, she didn't dare admit how much.

She raced for the door. With a yank, she pulled it open.

Her welcoming smile dissolved as painfully as if she'd been struck in the face by an acid bath. "Mr. Franklin?" she gasped in amazement.

"Young lady, I won't have you coming back into town to make trouble for me and my family."

His angry words pummeled her like the fists that had hurt her son. He was the same kind of bully, she thought. Fat and pompous, his hair was an unnatural shade of cinnamon brown that could only mean he had a cheap toupee and a huge case of vanity.

"I'm visiting my sister. You have no right—"

"That man you're hanging around with is no better than you are. He murdered my neice! If you two don't leave things as they are, I'll teach you both a lesson you won't soon forget." He shook a stubby finger in her face.

A red haze filled Marilee's vision. Taylor Franklin might still be making threats, but she wasn't listening. How long did a person have to live with injustice?

Only as long as she didn't fight back.

Chapter Six

She was mad as hell.

She'd fussed and fretted all night long. Nobody had a right to run her out of town. Last time she'd checked, Montana was still part of the good old U.S.A., a free country, and that included Newellton.

Her son had the right idea. With any luck, she could metaphorically get in a few good swings before she left town—in her own good time. It would serve Taylor Franklin right.

Turning off the county road, she headed up the drive to Luke's house. Granted, it wasn't the most prosperous ranch in the county, and the land wasn't the best around for grazing cattle, but there was a view that went clear into tomorrow. For somebody who'd spent the last thirteen years living in apartments where you were lucky to have a window facing the street, the panoramic scene was worth plenty.

As she marched up the rickety steps of Luke's front porch, she admitted the house was rundown. But it wasn't like the place was out of compliance with local building codes. It simply needed a little TLC to repair the damage done by too many harsh winters.

Evidently he'd heard her car because he opened the door before she had a chance to knock.

The sight of him standing behind the slightly out-of-kilter screen nearly took Marilee's breath away.

His sleep-mussed hair was all spiky, his jaw dark with morning whiskers. He was shirtless, and the broad chest she'd been so curious about boasted a cross of black curls, the vertical band of which slid out of sight beneath sinfully low-riding, faded jeans. The way the fly was worn and slightly frayed along the edge, straining across the bulge, conjured a thousand erotic images. Heated images she was powerless to quash.

"Kinda early for a neighborly call."

Her gaze snapped up. "I couldn't sleep."

In a lazy perusal, he studied her face, then let his eyes slip lower, to rest leisurely on her breasts before taking the measure of her hips and legs, encased in jeans far newer than his. Retracing the visual path he'd drawn at the same relaxed, heart-stopping pace, he asked, "You want some coffee?"

Coffee seemed a safer choice than what she was actually thinking about. "That would be nice."

She followed him into the kitchen where he snapped on the burner under the teakettle. Gooseflesh rose along her spine in response to a nervous shudder. She'd never been quite this alone with Luke.

Searching for some distraction, she spotted a crossword-puzzle magazine sitting open on the table, a stubby pencil marking the page he'd been working on. Mentally, she grabbed for the safety of something familiar and studied the clues.

"Nereis."

He turned. "What?"

"Nereis is the green worm they're looking for. Eleven across."

He cocked his head so he could see the page right side up and that wayward hank of hair slipped across his forehead. "You're right."

"I didn't know you did crosswords."

"It passes the time." He filled in the blanks. "You, too?"

Marilee suspected he'd done a thousand puzzles during eight years in prison. Maybe more.

"When I was getting my GED," she said, "there was a teacher who gave extra credit for doing crosswords. I got hooked." The exercise had filled all those lonely nights when she'd had only the TV and a crossword for company.

He glanced at the unfinished puzzle. "How 'bout a chronic disease? Starts with c."

"Cancer?"

"Too easy. It's eight letters."

"Would 'cachexia' fit?"

The corner of his mouth quirked. "You're good." He printed it, then looked up at her. "Somehow I don't think crossword puzzles were on your mind when you arrived.''

''Taylor Franklin came to see me after you left yesterday.''

''Is he somebody I'm supposed to know?''

''He's the mayor of Newellton...and Glen's grandfather.''

He nodded, as though he understood all the unpleasant implications of the relationship. ''He's giving you a hard time?''

''Evidently he thinks I'm here to make trouble for him—a belated effort at a paternity suit against his son.''

''You told him you weren't?''

''Taylor Franklin doesn't listen real well. He threatened to run me out of town.''

''You don't plan to stay long, anyway. I don't see there's a big problem.'' The kettle started to whistle, and Luke poured hot water into a mug already containing a generous teaspoonful of instant coffee. The mixture foamed.

''Taylor was also related to that girl who was killed in the hit-and-run. Says if you don't quit acting as if you're innocent, he's threatening dire consequences. He doesn't like ex-cons in *his* town.''

''Is that a fact?''

''He thinks eight years in prison wasn't nearly enough time for you to have served.'' She accepted the steaming mug he offered. ''I don't think he's making an idle threat, Luke. He seemed...furious.''

''Not long enough in prison?'' He gave a rough bark that was more curse than laugh. ''For the crime

I was supposed to have committed, I spent more time in prison than most. It was like somebody on the outside was trying to keep me locked up."

"Do you think it was Franklin? He's very influential in the county."

"If he was related to the victim..."

The thought of Taylor Franklin using his influence to hurt Luke, to keep him locked up behind prison walls a single minute longer than necessary, made Marilee sick to her stomach. "He's an easy man to hate."

"Don't waste your energy. I just wish he'd had enough nerve to tell me to my face how he feels instead of laying it all on you. Maybe I could have asked some pointed questions."

"That's exactly what I thought. He's always been an oversize bully." About three hundred pounds worth, based on his girth and jowls.

"So what are you going to do?"

"I'm going to stay in Newellton just as long as I want." She'd run away once, when Taylor Franklin had sent Bud out of state to school. She wasn't about to run away again. "And you and I are going to find out who was really driving the car that killed that girl."

Leaning back against the counter, Luke grinned. "What's a characteristic thought to be common among people with red hair? Six letters."

She bristled when the word he was seeking popped quickly to mind. "I'm very good at controlling my temper."

"Don't be on my account, particularly if the one you're mad at is this Taylor Franklin character. I've always wanted to have a woman defend me."

The heat of a blush raced up her cheeks.

"Truth is—" he shoved away from the counter as though nervous energy was making him restless "—the transcript didn't tell me a thing I didn't already know, and I've pretty well run out of leads. I don't know who to talk to next."

"Millie Russell."

"Why her?"

"She's a walking encyclopedia of Newellton."

"A couple of days ago she was ready to believe I'd murdered you and your son and stuffed you both in the trunk of your car. What makes you think she'd be willing to talk to us now?"

"Because it's genetically impossible for her to *stop* talking. Trust me, if she's heard the least little rumor, she'll tell us."

"What about Glen, Marilee? If you and I are seen together—"

"We aren't going to be in Newellton much longer. I don't think he's eager to go back into town anyway, not after those kids ganged up on him. He'll be all right." She'd make sure Glen gave the town of Newellton a wide berth, unless he was escorted by Hawk and a score of his deputies.

"Okay, you're the boss. Let me get a shirt on...." He stopped next to her on his way out of the kitchen, so close her fingers itched to explore the hair-roughened texture of his broad chest. Lowering his voice, he asked, "Was there any other reason besides

Franklin's threat that brought you clear out here so early in the morning?"

Oh, yes, there'd been a dozen other excuses she'd dreamed up during the night, most of them motivated by the memory of Luke's kiss, or the way she wanted to brush back that lock of hair that was forever sliding across his forehead. But those had been the mental gymnastics of a long-celibate woman troubled by a bad case of lust and were better left unsaid.

"Let's leave it at that for now," she hedged.

His big hands came up to gently cradle her face. "For now," he echoed with an unspoken promise. "Tell me, Ms. Haggerty, how is it I never met you when we were growing up? Newellton's a pretty small town."

She swallowed hard. If she'd known a man like Luke, her whole life might have been different. Or maybe she would have been even more foolish. "From what you've said, I think I'm a few years older than you are."

A smile played at the corners of his lips. "Ah, I've always wanted to get involved with an older woman."

Involved? No, that wasn't right. She'd come to Luke's house to help a friend and to get back at Taylor Franklin. That's all. She didn't dare consider any other possibility. It was better for all concerned for her to keep her heart safely under lock and key. A permanent relationship with an ex-con, even one who was innocent, was entirely out of the question. Look what it had already cost her son.

"Hiya, toots! Wanna smooch?"

Marilee stared at the parrot sitting on his perch next

to the window. Surely the silly bird hadn't winked at her.

Carrying a tray with cookies and mugs of hot apple cider, Mrs. Russell reappeared from the kitchen. There'd been no way to discourage her hospitality. And frankly, the smell of freshly baked cookies had been more temptation than either Luke or Marilee could resist. The scent of cinnamon and apples added to the mix of pleasant aromas in the cozy living room, which boasted overstuffed chairs and a welcoming fireplace.

"Now that you've tweaked my memory," Mrs. Russell said, setting the tray on the table next to Marilee, "I do remember there was some whispering after poor little Joanie was killed. The whole town was grieving, as you can well imagine. Such a shock to lose a child so young. Just fifteen, I think. Then, when the sheriff…that's not Sheriff Hawk, you understand, but the one before him. Sheriff Ramsey. Such a good man. He retired just before his wife—"

"Mrs. Russell, could you tell us more about what you heard after the accident?" Marilee asked.

"Yes, dear." She handed Luke his cup. "My, how I remember you riding that motorcycle of yours. You could make it stand on end just like a circus performer. Came right up on the sidewalk once. Nearly scared me out of ten years of my life, and I can't afford to waste a one at my age."

"I'm sorry, Mrs. Russell. Could we get back to—"

Squawk! "*Charlie wants a cookie!*" The bird hopped from his perch to the table.

Marilee rolled her eyes. Keeping the conversation on track was like trying to put up a fence in quicksand.

"Of course, dear." Mrs. Russell offered Marilee a cookie, then held the plate out for Luke to make a selection. They were thick chocolate chip cookies with nuts, a traditional recipe that brought back memories of Marilee's childhood, when Mrs. Russell and Grandma Claire had been friends visiting back and forth across the street. "I was saying that Joanie was killed not all that far from Lovers Gulch. You probably remember the place?" the elderly woman sent Luke a questioning look.

"Vaguely." A surprising splash of color tinged his ruddy complexion, and Marilee stifled a laugh. She remembered Lovers Gulch herself. Perhaps too clearly.

"We all thought it was odd that little Joanie was walking along the edge of the road so late at night that far out of town. But then, who's to know what teenagers are thinking? She was supposed to have been at a girlfriend's house for a slumber party."

"Which girlfriend?"

"Well now, I'm not sure I remember...." The woman broke off a piece of cookie for Charlie, then shooed him back to his perch.

"*Land ho!*" Holding the cookie in his claw, he daintily began to eat.

"I did hear she'd been dating Andy Martins. He was a little older than Joanie, sixteen or seventeen. Nothing steady, I gathered. More off than on, I was told. But his folks swore he'd been home all that night, so she couldn't have been out to Lovers Gulch with him."

"Unless his parents lied," Luke muttered under his breath.

"And Andy's license had already been suspended for too many speeding tickets, so his parents wouldn't have loaned him their car. They're good people. Solid citizens in the community, just like Jake is. Fine family."

"The opposite of Luke and his father," Marilee interjected with a touch of sarcasm.

"Oh, my..." Mrs. Russell rearranged the few items on the tray. "I guess we were all relieved when they decided you were the one who had killed that girl, Luke. You had quite a reputation, you know."

"Yeah. But what if they were so eager to point a finger at me, the town troublemaker, that they let the guilty guy go free?"

The color drained from Mrs. Russell's face and she was actually quiet for a moment. Thoughtfully quiet.

"Wanna come up to my place, babe?"

Marilee frowned trying to ignore the parrot. Wherever had Mrs. Russell gotten that ridiculous bird?

"Why don't I package up some of these cookies for your boy, Marilee? If I know teenagers, he probably has a sweet tooth. Home baking—"

"That's all right, Mrs. Russell." Marilee stood. "We should be going."

"One more question." Luke placed his cup on the tray. "Do you have any idea where Andy Martins is now?"

"No, I don't think I do." Millie Russell shook her head. "Odd, isn't it? I haven't heard Jake mention that boy in years. They used to be so close and now...it's like he vanished from the face of the earth."

Marilee suspected she knew why. Keeping secrets put stress on any family relationship.

"You know a five-letter word signifying falsehood?" Luke asked.

"You think Mrs. Russell is lying?"

"Maybe not, but Jake is. Everybody else has suspicions, but only Jake knows for sure. And Andy, who isn't about to show his face again in Newellton."

They were still sitting in Luke's truck, parked across the street from Mrs. Russell's house and right in front of the home where Marilee had grown up. Mrs. Russell had said a young couple was living there now. They were expecting their first child in the summer.

New beginnings.

Marilee was dragging along so much baggage from the past, she wondered if she'd ever have a chance for a new beginning. Luke seemed to be in the same boat.

"That's where you used to live?" he asked, following her gaze.

"Yes. My biggest regret is that I hurt Grandma Claire when I ran away, and I never even told her I was sorry. Now it's too late. She died a couple of years ago."

"It's okay, babe. My guess is she understood you were doing the best you could. She probably knew you had to find your own way in life and just hoped you'd be all right."

With his arm resting along the back of the seat, he toyed with the hair at her nape, those strands that refused to stay in place however carefully she combed them. She wished he wouldn't do that. And hoped he'd never stop.

His fingers settled on the back of her neck. Based on the heat she felt—almost as though she was being branded—Marilee suspected he had a raging metabolism. A perfect man to curl up with on a cold winter's night.

"Do you ever let your hair down?" His voice was low and raspy, roughly intimate in the close confines of the truck.

She forced herself to breathe evenly. "Only at night. It's not very well behaved."

"Like Glen's?"

"Not quite that bad."

He stroked the back of his fingers along the column of her neck, demonstrating an uncanny ability to find the most sensitive spot. Or maybe anywhere he touched her would respond with the same leap of desire.

"Some day—or some night," he promised, "I'd like to be the one to pull those pins out and let your hair down."

Her heart fluttered at the thought, even though she was going to object to his suggestion. The words were right there on the tip of her tongue to deny the possibility, but before she could speak, his mouth covered hers. Softly. Warmly. Silencing her.

When she gasped, he erased all memory of her objection with the sweep of his tongue across hers. Sweet, rough velvet. Hot and moist. She almost cried aloud at the pleasure that shot through her. He shouldn't be doing this. Not here. Not in broad daylight. And not in Newellton, on the street where she'd grown up.

As he broke the kiss, she caught a glimpse of movement across the street—the lace curtain shifting in Millie Russell's window—and she mentally groaned. Their kiss would be the talk of the town before they were halfway down the block.

"I think we'd better go," she murmured. Though there was no way they could outrun the gossip.

"How 'bout Lovers Gulch?" he teased. "We could check out the scene of the crime."

She flushed, knowing darn well he wasn't thinking about investigating anything except on an intimate level. "I think we're a little old for that. Particularly in the middle of the day."

He gave her one of those heavy-lidded looks that encouraged a woman to suggest they head to the nearest bedroom. "Yeah, I guess."

Breaking the spell, Luke shifted position and started the truck. "After I take you back to your car, I'm going to talk to a realtor. Thought I'd better see how much I can get for the ranch."

It took Marilee a moment to catch up with his abrupt switch in topics. Her mind was still locked on the image of them in bed together, her body responding and melting in a fundamentally feminine way to his every touch.

Luke got a call that afternoon asking him to show up at Hawk's house after dinner. The caller, a female deputy sheriff, was not particularly friendly. Luke figured the news, whatever it was, wouldn't be good.

When he arrived, Marilee answered the door.

During eight years in prison, Luke had learned to have no illusions and damn few dreams. Yet a thousand images leapt into his mind at the sight of Marilee holding Beth's baby in her arms.

He'd forgotten how much a man wanted to find a nurturing woman to give him a child of his own. That wasn't what you thought about behind bars. Instead, you kept track of the man walking behind you, in case he had filed his spoon into a shiv and had reason to shove it between your shoulder blades.

You thought about women in general and sex in particular. A lot. But you didn't think much about how soft a child's hair was or how good it felt to be welcomed by a smiling woman whose skin would be even sweeter to touch than a baby's.

If Luke had good sense, he wouldn't be thinking about those dreams now while he was wide awake. An ex-con had nothing to offer a woman like Marilee. He could ache for her all day and all night, but it wouldn't do him a damn bit of good.

"Hawk said I was to stop by," he said, valiantly trying to quash the unfamiliar tender feelings that welled up in him.

"I know. He called to say he'd be late." She opened the door wider. "Beth wasn't feeling well, so I sent her to bed for a nap. That way I get to play auntie." Smiling, she squeezed the baby, who dropped her head to Marilee's shoulder.

"Where's Glen?" Luke walked past them into the living room, catching the faint scent of baby powder.

"He's in Beth's studio creating a robot man—or something equally macho—in watercolors. He inherited some of her talent, I think."

A lump formed in Luke's chest as he watched the baby snuggle in Marilee's arms. "You look real natural. Holding a baby, I mean."

"It's been a long time. I guess it's something you never forget."

"I've never been around kids much." Not a one had dropped by his cell for a visit, he thought wryly. "I wouldn't know how to act."

"You want to hold her?"

Before he could object, Marilee had extended Sarah toward him. To Luke's surprise, the baby held out her arms. Now how could a guy refuse an invitation like that?

Awkwardly, he hooked his arm under her bottom. "Whata ya think, munchkin?" She grabbed his nose and twisted. "Hey, take it easy. That's mine."

Marilee laughed, a light sound that reminded Luke of champagne bubbling in a crystal glass. She ought to laugh more often, he thought. Her eyes sparkled when she did.

"See? She's already quite taken with you. You must have a way with women."

"Maybe with babies and women over eighty," he conceded. The baby's finger slipped into his mouth, and he nibbled lightly. Her dark eyes studied him intently.

"A few in between might be interested, too."

He slid his gaze from Sarah, to lock with Marilee's green eyes. "Maybe they'd be interested until they learned I'm an ex-con. Not many women would want anything to do with a man who'd spent time in prison."

He saw the denial reach her lips, but she didn't say the words. They would have been a lie. Both of them knew an ex-con wasn't the catch of the decade. With Marilee's past, she would be particularly leery of a guy who could bring trouble down on her kid. Smart lady.

As though embarrassed that she hadn't disagreed with his assessment, she fussed with the hem of little Sarah's skirt. "So what did they tell you at the real-estate office?"

"Some guy is going to check the bank records, then come out to take a look around. Gave me some mumbo jumbo about the market being slow, prices down. I figure that's so he can make a quick deal and rip me off in the process."

"You can always get a second opinion. Mayor Franklin is in the real-estate business," she suggested with feigned innocence.

Luke's sudden rough laugh startled the baby. She closed her eyes, opened her mouth and let out a full-size squall.

"Hey, munchkin, don't do that! I didn't mean to scare you," Luke murmured joggling her up and down gently in his arms.

She squirmed and extended her arms to Marilee anyway, in a desperate effort to escape.

"Here, I'll take her."

"Another fickle woman," Luke grumbled, passing Sarah to her aunt. Immediately, he missed having the infant in his arms, and the sensation surprised him. When had he started thinking so much about kids and family?

From the back of the house, Hawk called, "Anybody home?" As he came into the living room, he tossed his Stetson on a chair. "Sorry I'm late. We never seem to have a crisis in the middle of the day."

Sarah identified her daddy as the savior she'd been waiting for and upped the decibel level until he lifted her into his arms.

The swift blade of envy sliced through Luke. Raymond Hawk was a damn lucky man.

Eventually things quieted down. Beth came out of the bedroom to serve Hawk the meal she'd kept warm in the oven and to retrieve her now-sleepy daughter. After giving her husband a quick kiss, she carried the baby off to bed.

Luke and Marilee sat down at the kitchen table with Hawk. He took a couple of bites of pot roast before he said, "I've had some of my people checking back through the records on your case, Luke. Something has turned up."

"Yeah?" Luke hoped it was Andy Martins's confession, but supposed that was unlikely.

Hawk glanced from Luke to Marilee and back again, his expression not giving much away. "There was an ATM robbery in Harlowton the night Joanie Tarkington was killed. Harlowton is in the next county, which is another jurisdiction, and that's why the two crimes weren't connected before now."

"You're saying they should have been connected?" Luke asked.

"It's possible. The bank's surveillance camera picked up a partial license plate on the car we think belonged to the perpetrator. From what we can see, that car and the one we know was involved in the hit-and-run could have been the same vehicle."

"But you don't know that for sure."

Hawk stabbed a piece of potato with his fork, put it into his mouth and chewed thoughtfully. "Not unequivocally. The investigators in that crime interviewed the victim, a seventy-year-old woman who had been knocked down from behind. She provided a rather sketchy description of the perp."

Tension tightened in Luke's gut.

"She said the robber had been tall—maybe six feet—and slender. Probably on the young side. He was wearing jeans, a T-shirt and a black cowboy hat." Hawk's eyes narrowed. "Did you ever own a black Stetson, Luke?"

Marilee gave an audible gasp and bit her lower lip. Luke realized she knew damn well he had a black hat. She'd seen him wear it more than once.

"I still own one, Sheriff. Me and half the men in Montana, I'd guess, plus just as many in every other state in the West."

"True enough," Hawk conceded.

"Luke's been in jail eight years for a crime he didn't commit," Marilee said. "Surely you're not going to accuse him of this robbery, too."

"No one's making any accusations at this point. Since the crime had never been solved, my counterpart in Harlowton has reopened the investigation. So far, that's all that's happened. I thought Luke would want to know."

"So I can skip town?" The sharp taste of bitter memories rose in Luke's throat. He was the guy they all wanted to convict. The patsy who'd taken the fall for someone else. "Isn't there a statute of limitations on robbery?"

"All I'm saying is that the case is under renewed investigation."

Hawk's words penetrated Luke's brain like a stiletto. If someone back then had wanted him locked up for a long time, maybe they still did. This new case would be the perfect chance to railroad him a second time. All because he'd wanted to clear his name.

He flexed his fingers into fists, and a muscle twitched at his jaw. *Not this time!*

Chapter Seven

Marilee grabbed her jacket and followed Luke out to his truck. He'd left the house in a controlled rage. She didn't want him to do anything foolish, commit an act guaranteed to send him back to prison. The possibility terrified her.

"We could talk to Andy's parents," she suggested, hurrying to catch up with him.

He kept striding down the walkway, every step underscoring his anger. "You think they're going blow the whistle on their son and confess they lied to the cops eight years ago? Not a chance in hell."

"Maybe Joanie's girlfriends know something. We could ask—"

"Marilee, it's no good. Somebody wants me back in prison."

"Franklin?" Her voice caught on the name—her son's own flesh and blood, his grandfather. Could anyone be that cruel?

"Maybe a whole lot of folks do." Luke braced his hands against the top of the truck cab. Tension radiated from him like an overloaded transformer about to explode. "You know a six-letter synonym for Luke Spurwood? *Sucker!*"

She felt his pain twisting through her heart, and knew the bravery it took to even try to make a joke. He was such a good man. More caring than he would want to admit. Gentle in spite of all the hard times he'd survived, showing bitterness because he was too strong to reveal any weakness.

She placed her hand on his arm, to soothe and calm. Instead, his heat and energy arced through her, the current sending a burning shiver down her spine.

He turned and dragged her into his arms. Roughly. Hungrily. "God, I wish I could forget all about that damn hit-and-run, the girl who died, the robbery—everything."

He held her so tightly she could barely draw a breath, yet she cherished the feeling of the hard length of his body pressed against hers, the way he held her in the firm nest of his hips. His breath warmed her temple. Beneath her palm, his heart beat with a rapid pulse that matched her own frantic response.

Above them the stars had begun to appear, the night sky draping the landscape in an intimate cloak of deep velvet. Only at the farthest reaches of hearing did the sound of a single car on the highway intrude.

Marilee's hands crept up Luke's shoulders, slipping to the back of his neck, where her fingers twined through the long, silken strands of his hair. His mouth claimed hers in an erotic kiss, feasting as their tongues tangled together. Exploring. Promising more.

Deftly, he plucked the pins that held her staid coil of hair in place. The released weight settled sensuously across her shoulders, and she trembled.

"Oh, God, Marilee," he groaned. "I want to take you home. I want to take you upstairs to that big bed you slept in and make love to you until there's only the two of us, the rest of the world be damned!"

Temptation sizzled through her at his shockingly desperate plea. She had the insane urge to agree. To hop into his truck and let him take her wherever he wanted. Do whatever he wanted.

Because she wanted it, too.

But she'd practiced caution for the past fourteen years, until the habit was well ingrained. No matter how much she was attracted to Luke, he was the wrong man. This was the wrong place. For them, there might never be a right time. She didn't dare leap into an intimate relationship before she was confident of the depth of his feelings. And hers.

The whispered refusal formed painfully in her throat. "I can't."

"Why not? Are you afraid of me, an ex-con? Or yourself?"

"No. You don't understand. It's too soon for us to—"

"Look, I've been in prison for eight years. That's a helluva long time. I don't need some woman telling me it's too soon to make love."

Cold flooded all those needy places that moments ago had been warmed by the heated flash of desire. "Is that all you want me for? To make up for eight years of not having a woman?"

"Dammit, that's not what I meant." Releasing her, he speared his fingers through his hair. His lips were set in a grim line, his jaw tight. "I'm sorry, okay? I'm a little upset by what Hawk said, that's all. I shouldn't have taken my frustration out on you."

"Hey, Mom! Are you out there?"

Marilee jumped as if she'd been struck by a cattle prod. "I'd better go in. Glen probably wants to show me his painting."

"Yeah. Right. I'll call you tomorrow."

Without responding, Marilee raced for the house. She scrubbed the back of her hand against her eyes. There was no need for her son to see her crying. No need for anyone to realize how vulnerable Luke made her feel.

An hour ago she'd been thinking what a wonderful father he'd make. And how much she'd like to have his baby.

Obviously, he only had sex on his mind. Just like Bud.

He'd blown it.

Slamming the posthole digger into ground muddy from the spring thaw, Luke cursed himself. He'd come on too strong last night. Scared Marilee half to death. Little wonder she'd panicked.

He'd seen the fear in her eyes, felt the anxious tremble ripple through her body. She was afraid of him. Luke Spurwood. Ex-con.

If he had any sense, he'd drive over to the county seat, find a woman who'd ease the terrible ache in his groin for a few bucks and be done with it. But he didn't want that kind of woman. He never had. And he knew, even if he succumbed to that kind of temptation, it wouldn't do him a damn bit of good.

He wanted Marilee Haggerty. And he was all wrong for her. He didn't have anything more to offer her now than he'd had when the blizzard blew her into his life. Now he might even be sent back to prison.

So he struggled to work out his frustrations by fixing a fence he didn't give a damn about. Physical exertion had always helped. Until now.

He looked up to see Glen peddling Hawk's bike up the road. For an instant he let himself think about having a son like Glen, then he shoved the thought aside. How could a boy look up to a father who'd done eight years of hard time?

That'd be about as bad as having an old man who was a drunk.

"Hey, Luke, what's up?" Glen let his earphones drop to his shoulders.

"Not much."

He slid the bike to a stop on the gravel shoulder. He was breathing hard from the last mile or so of gentle grade. "What are you doing?"

"Mending fences." And giving himself a few well-deserved mental kicks in the butt.

"Can I help?"

Luke hauled another mound of dirt from the hole. "You strong enough to bring me one of those fence posts from the back of the truck?"

"Sure." Dropping the bike to the ground, Glen loped to the truck. The return trip went a little slower. "Where do you want it?"

"Let 'er slid right into the hole." Kids Glen's age needed to know they could handle a man's job, so Luke stood back while the boy wrestled with the post. "Good job," he said when the post finally wobbled into place.

Glen grinned. "That sucker was heavy."

"I know." He tipped his hat farther back on his head, eyeing the youngster. "Why do you think I let you handle it?"

The boy's whoop of laughter made Luke smile. He couldn't remember ever laughing with his old man when they were working together. He'd been all gruff and grumble, showing little affection after his wife had died. Luke had only been about ten at the time. He liked the feel of this easy camaraderie with Marilee's son.

Kicking a clod of dirt with his toe, Glen asked, "Did you and Mom have a fight last night or somethin'?"

"Why do you ask?"

"She seemed upset, is all. I thought maybe..." He lifted his narrow shoulders in an awkward shrug.

"Your mother's a good woman." Too good for an ex-con who had the hots for her, a guy somebody wanted to see put back behind bars.

"You like her, don't you?"

"I think that's between me and your mom."

Glen scuffed his toe again, avoiding eye contact with Luke. "I think she likes you."

"Hey, what is this? You trying to play match-maker?"

"Naw, it's just that . . . it wouldn't be so bad to live on a ranch. If you had a satellite dish, I mean."

Luke felt like he'd been hit in the chest. The kid was taking a shot at finding himself a father, and he was looking in exactly the wrong place. Regret slid through him. Luke Spurwood didn't have the qualifications for the job.

"Come on, runt." He hooked Glen in a playful headlock, mostly so the kid wouldn't see how his words had affected him. "If we're going to get this fence looking like something besides a string of drunken sailors, we gotta get humping."

"You're not mad at what I said?"

"Hell, no. To prove it, I'll let you dig the next hole."

"Mrs. Franklin, I can't think of a thing we have to say to each other."

"You're the mother of my grandson. Surely we can find some common ground."

Marilee folded her arms across her chest. Silver haired and looking like she'd just come from the beauty shop, Glen's grandmother was the top of whatever social ladder existed in Newellton—president of the Newellton Garden Club, secretary of the Women's Philanthropic Association, an elder in her church. She'd served on governors' advisory boards and had once been invited to Washington, D.C. She was definitely the power behind Mayor Franklin's very small throne. That the woman would come to Beth's house to speak with Marilee was more than a surprise. She was grateful Glen was off visiting Luke at his ranch.

Marilee hadn't let Isabelle Franklin in the house. They stood instead on the front porch, a brisk spring breeze chilling the air and fluttering Mrs. Franklin's skirt.

"You weren't very interested in discussing common ground fourteen years ago," Marilee replied quietly.

"My dear, Taylor and my son managed to keep me in the dark about your, ah...your *pregnancy*." Otherwise self-assured, she stumbled over the word.

"In a town that thrives on gossip? That's hard to believe."

"Nonetheless, it's true."

Lacing her voice with sarcasm, Marilee said, "I suppose if you had known, you would have happily paid for my bus fare out of town."

Isabelle Franklin blanched. "Certainly not. I would have made Bud accept responsibility for his indiscretion."

God, how Marilee hated having her son thought of as an "indiscretion." "His name is Glen," she said through clenched teeth.

"Yes, of course. He's also the only grandson I'll ever have."

"Bud married. He had children."

"Three girls. They're lovely, really lovely. But after he died, their mother took them to Seattle to be with her family." In spite of Isabelle's obvious effort to control her emotions, her chin trembled. "I miss them terribly. I was hoping... You see, I thought it might be possible for Taylor and me to get acquainted with your Glen. Every child needs grandparents."

"Your husband doesn't seem to think so. He's been trying to run me out of town."

"Surely you must have misunderstood. Taylor can get a bit blustery, I admit. Bud always was his Achilles' heel, but he wouldn't take our loss out on you and the boy."

The temper Marilee had been so often accused of having boiled near the surface. "Mrs. Franklin, I can't imagine my son wanting a grandfather who is so vindictive that he would keep an innocent man in jail longer than necessary and then try to send him back to prison on another trumped-up charge."

Her eyes widened. "I have no idea what you're talking about."

"Luke Spurwood. The mayor has taken a special interest in his case, along with trying to run me and my son out of town."

"Oh, my..." Clearly taken by surprise, Mrs. Franklin fussed with the clutch purse she carried. "Taylor was terribly upset when Joanie died. Her death devastated him. She was his favorite niece, you see."

"I see a man who misuses his influence."

"Perhaps he has been overly conscientious in pursuing justice."

"Luke's only crime was being a little wild. The fine folks of Newellton gave him eight years in prison to settle down." Just as she had spent fourteen years in exile atoning for her sins.

With a slow nod of her head, Mrs. Franklin considered Marilee's position. "*If* I were able to convince my husband that he should not pursue the case further, would you at least consider the possibility of allowing us to meet our grandson?"

Tit for tat. An interesting possibility. No wonder Mrs. Franklin had been valued as a constituent by the past three Montana governors. She'd extended an offer difficult to refuse, particularly when it meant removing the threat of another term in prison for Luke.

"I would consider asking Glen how he feels about meeting you," Marilee agreed.

The tension left Mrs. Franklin's shoulders and she smiled. "Thank you, Ms. Haggerty. I deeply appreciate the sacrifices you have made for your son."

Marilee doubted anyone could fully comprehend the difficulties she'd faced in those early years unless they had lived through a similar experience. In some way, however, Mrs. Franklin's acknowledgment dulled the sharp edge of painful memories.

Mrs. Franklin's big Cadillac had barely vanished out of sight when Luke's truck appeared, coming down the road from the opposite direction. He took the turn into Hawk's driveway too fast, and gravel spewed from the back tires.

Excitement and fear vied for dominance in Marilee's stomach. She had planned to avoid seeing Luke during the rest of her stay in Newellton. Stubbornly, she had tamped down the urge to do just as he had wanted—go to his ranch and march up those narrow stairs to the master bedroom. Into Luke's arms. Her body thrummed with the knowledge of how much she desired him.

But a greater instinct—a well-honed maternal instinct—won the battle.

Her son! Glen was with Luke. And Luke was driving as through there was an emergency. With the sun glinting off the windshield, Marilee couldn't see if there was a passenger in the truck.

She raced down the walkway to the drive. Before the vehicle came to a full stop, she yanked open the door.

"Hey, Mom. What's up?"

Her breath lingered in her lungs for several heavy heartbeats before she was able to exhale. "Are you all right?"

"Sure." Nonchalantly, Glen hopped down and went to the back to haul his bike out of the truck bed.

She whirled on Luke, who'd come around to her side of the vehicle. "What in the world do you think you're doing? You scared the liver out of me, driving like a madman. I thought Glen had been hurt!" Or worse. Dear Lord, she'd pictured him broken and bloodied.

"Jake's had a heart attack."

The images in her mind shifted and rearranged themselves into a picture of an aging garage mechanic lying in a casket.

"The hospital called me," Luke continued. "Jake's asking to see me."

"He's still alive?"

"Yeah. For the moment. His condition's critical." He reached for her, as though he was going to brush a straying bit of hair away from her face, then he dropped his hand to his side. "Look, I know I acted stupid last night. I came on too strong and I didn't mean to."

"It's water under the bridge." She shrugged and shot Glen a glance. He'd gotten the bike out of the truck and was walking toward the garage, well out of earshot.

"I still want you, don't get me wrong—"

An unbidden cry of "Hallelujah!" rose in her throat.

"—But right now I need you to come with me to the hospital."

She did another mental turnaround. "What for?"

"The only reason Jake would be asking for me is if he's finally going to tell the truth. He's going to clear me, Marilee. I know he is. I want you there with me."

That seemed reasonable. They'd interviewed all the other possible sources of information together. She'd heard Millie Russell come just short of implicating

Andy Martins. Logic demanded Marilee be there when all the cards were finally spread faceup on the table.

Her heart eagerly went along with the plan. She wanted to see Luke vindicated almost as much as he did.

Chapter Eight

Excitement hummed in Luke's chest. As he turned left out of the elevator, Marilee caught his arm. "They said he's in the Cardiac Intensive Care Unit." She pointed to the arrow on the wall.

"Yeah, right." Distracted, he changed course to follow her lead. He felt like a kid waiting for Santa Claus and scared to death he wouldn't show up.

Every couple of paces, late-afternoon sunlight splashed through a window into the subdued gray hallway. Luke knew he'd gotten excited before—about paroles refused and work releases denied—but nothing had counted as much as this—proof positive that he never should have been convicted at all. *Don't die, Jake. Not till you've told the truth.* He'd been repeating those words like a mantra during the entire drive from Newellton to the county hospital.

"You sure they'll let you see him?" Marilee asked. "You're not a relative."

"The nurse said he'd been making such a fuss, the doctor gave permission."

The hallway widened to allow room for a couple of hard-looking couches and a coffee table spilling over with dog-eared magazines. An elderly woman, probably the wife of a patient, looked up as they arrived, then glanced away, as if she'd been hoping to see someone else. A son or daughter, Luke imagined. Someone to hold her hand while she waited word on the fate of her husband.

A closed door blocked the entrance to the CICU. Luke tried it, but it was locked.

"You have to talk to the nurses through the intercom," the woman explained. "They only let you in once every hour. Then you can only stay—" she gave a small sob "—for ten minutes."

Not a long time to hear the truth, Luke thought. Or to say goodbye. He wondered when he reached old age if there'd be anyone there to give a damn.

He punched the intercom button. The seconds ticked silently by while he waited. Impatience had him on edge, and he pressed the button again.

An unintelligible female voice responded.

He answered the question he assumed had been asked. "Luke Spurwood to see Jake Martins."

More time passed. He felt like he was waiting to mount a gallows stairs, not waiting to be set free of the past.

The door clicked open. A woman in white shot him a look, then slid a disapproving gaze in Marilee's direction.

"She's with me," Luke said.

The nurse gave a reluctant nod.

The way Marilee slipped her arm through his bolstered Luke's courage. She was a strong woman. She'd raised her kid and gotten her life together all on her own. He tried to absorb some of her strength through the warmth that radiated from her small, delicate fingers resting at the crook of his arm.

Inside the double doors, recessed fixtures diffused the light, encouraging quiet exchanges of medical information among the personnel at the nurses' station and those walking silently on rubber-soled shoes. Glass windows allowed views into the various rooms. Monitors chirped and ticked like crickets on a summer evening.

Luke began to sweat. God, he hated hospitals. He remembered his mother dying in one. Remembered the smell of antiseptic and death. Then his father had started a binge that had lasted until he died, six months ago. His old man had found sobriety the hard way.

"Try not to be disappointed if this doesn't work out like you want," Marilee warned.

"The only reason he'd ask to see me is because of his conscience." Luke couldn't accept any other possibility. Not now. Not when he was so close to clearing his name.

"Here he is," the nurse announced. "Remember, you can't stay long."

When they stepped into Jake's room, Luke was struck by the transience of human life. Never robust in appearance, the old man now looked gray, his wrinkles as deeply etched in his narrow cheeks as the grooves in a new tire. An assortment of wires linked him to a monitor, the green line moving in steady peaks and valleys across the screen.

"He looks like he's asleep," Marilee whispered. "Maybe we shouldn't bother him."

"It's now or never."

Jake's eyes fluttered open, unfocused at first and then settling on Luke. "You came." He sighed. He coughed, and the green line on the monitor spiked.

"I thought it might be important."

He worked his mouth and licked chapped lips. "I did you a real disservice, boy."

"I've guessed as much."

"I should have said somethin' years ago. Can you forgive an old man?"

Could he? Luke wasn't sure. Eight years was a helluva price to pay for somebody else's crime. "I just want the record set straight."

Tears formed in the old man's eyes. "I've taken care of things. At the shop...got to worrying since you come back. It's safe...." His voice slurred. "I—I loved Andy like he was my own. You understand, don't you?"

"I'm trying." Luke's gut twisted with the burning need to have his innocence acknowledged, particularly in front of Marilee. He wanted to remove the last of her doubts. "Would you talk to Sheriff Hawk? Tell him the truth?"

"Hawk's a good man. He'd understand. It'd be nice to have him visit." The light faded from his eyes. "You ask him to drop by, eh?"

Oh, yeah, Luke would take care of that. He'd send the FBI, the CIA and anybody else he could think of to witness a statement that he hadn't killed that poor little girl.

"I'll see to it, Jake."

"Andy wasn't a bad boy."

"I know, Jake. I know." A coward, maybe. A kid with a temper who'd been told to get lost by some girl when he'd been planning to get into her pants out at Lovers Gulch. But not necessarily bad. Or maybe he'd had lousy depth perception and had only meant to scare her, coming too close with the car he'd stolen. Only Andy could tell them for sure—if they ever found him.

The nurse stuck her head through the door. "Time's up. Mr. Martins needs his rest."

"Right." Luke took the old man's hand. The telltale stains of fifty years as a mechanic lingered under his fingernails and in the ridges of his calluses. "I'll send Sheriff Hawk around."

"You do that, boy." Fatigue weighed Jake's eyelids.

Marilee pulled her lower lip between her teeth, trying to halt the quiver in her chin. It didn't do much good. She was so darn happy for Luke. When bad things happened, she got stubborn and fought back, but the joy in life always brought tears to her eyes.

She sensed Luke hadn't had much happiness—certainly not since he'd been sent to jail. He deserved this moment.

When they got back to the hallway outside the CICU, Luke exploded like a bottle of champagne finally uncorked.

"Did you hear that, Merry Mari?" Grinning, he lifted her off her feet and spun her around, twirling down the corridor with her until she felt as intoxicated as he was. "I'm free! Really free! Nobody's going to get me for that robbery. Nobody's going to send me back to jail. I'm a free man. The cops were wrong. Dead wrong!"

"Shh! This is a hospital." Her own loud laughter contradicted her warning.

"I don't care." Breathlessly, he whirled them to a halt in front of the elevators. "I want to shout it from the rooftops. Those jerks had the wrong guy all along. Jake will tell 'em! The old guy is gonna come through."

"That's what he says."

Luke's eyes sparkled and squint lines deepened at the corners. "We gotta celebrate. Big-time!"

Dancing them into the empty elevator, he caught her face between his hands. "Tomorrow night. I'm gonna get me some fancy duds and we're going out to paint the town. Whata ya say?"

How could she resist? She'd never seen a man so happy. The darkness that had always lurked just below the surface of Luke's hooded good looks had vanished, replaced with a boyish enthusiasm that was contagious. But last night he'd only had sex on his mind. Would he—or any man—ever want her for more than a quick tumble?

Doubts and years of insecurities chilled her into silence.

"I'll be on my best behavior," he promised, as though reading her mind. He held up his right hand, palm forward. "I swear. I won't even so much as kiss you." His mock seriousness broke up as he flashed her another smile. "Of course, I can't promise not to think about it a little."

She laughed. What else could she do? With his wicked grin, Luke was more tempting than ever. Or maybe in her heart she wanted him to be a noble hero, someone pure and good who could counter her own foolish past.

He leaned forward, his lips only a fraction of an inch from hers. "Say yes, Merry Mari," he cajoled in a far-too-persuasive whisper. "Help me celebrate."

Her acceptance slipped from her lips before she could drag it back. "Yes, I'll go out with you."

Her heart gave a wild tumble in response to his victorious smile. Then the elevator door opened at the lobby level, depositing them into the middle of a shouting match.

"Whata ya mean, we can't see our buddy?" Wearing a leather jacket emblazoned with the gang logo Vipers and carrying a motorcycle helmet, one man stood nose-to-nose with the hospital security officer.

"Your friend is in the emergency room. Our policy is to allow no visitors except family members."

"Yeah, so? Maybe I'm his brother."

A second disreputable-looking man stepped up, this one with dirty blond dreadlocks and arms covered in tattoos. "And I'm his dear ol' dad. We wanta see Caveman."

Caveman? Marilee cringed at the image the name conjured up.

The security officer spoke into his hand-held radio without taking his eyes off the troublemakers. "You've been barred from this hospital entirely. If you'll leave your name and a number where you can be reached—"

The first man grabbed the officer by his lapel. "Some juicehead ran our buddy off the road. We wanta—"

To Marilee's shock and horror, Luke stepped into the middle of the argument.

"Take it easy, Diablo. This isn't a cell block, and the locals don't take kindly to being pushed around."

Diablo turned on Luke as if he was going to smash him in the face, then his angry expression slowly shifted into one of pleasure. "Son of gun. Spurs! My ol' buddy! What the hell are you doing here?"

"Visiting a friend, just like you."

Luke hooked his arm around the burly stranger, his voice lowering enough that Marilee couldn't hear his words as he walked his friend away from the security officer. But before they had gone far, two other uniformed men arrived, both of them armed. Outside, the flashing light of a police car flicked across the windows.

Within moments, Diablo, his buddy and Luke—aka Spurs—had been forcefully ushered toward the door.

"No, wait!" Marilee cried. "He isn't one of them."

But he was, she realized, as he was shoved up against the patrol car, made to stand feet apart with arms outstretched, and frisked. He went through the motions effortlessly, without the slightest objection, as though the same thing had happened to him a hundred times in the past. It probably had.

Innocent or not, Luke would always be caught in the tangled net of his past. Just as Marilee had been snared by her own reckless behavior. The thought made her sick to her stomach.

There was still no way she dared risk her heart with someone whose reputation was far worse than her own. If she ever chose a man to be a father for her son, Glen deserved to have one who was above reproach. Her own imperfect past, engendering the gossip and knowing looks it did, was enough of a burden for a young boy to carry. Even in a new town, people were sure to suspect Glen had been born out of wedlock.

But that didn't mean she'd let Luke get hauled off to the hoosegow by some baby-faced cop.

She pushed her way past a couple of bystanders and right up to the policeman who was interrogating Luke. "Officer, I believe there's been a mistake. Mr. Spurwood was attempting to diffuse a tense situation. I'm sure if you check—"

"Ma'am, you'll have to stay back."

"But I'm trying to explain—"

"Lady, if you don't get back on the sidewalk I'll have to arrest you along with these men for disturbing the peace."

"Marilee, leave it alone," Luke warned.

"Quiet down, mister," the officer ordered. "Move it, lady."

"I'm a law-abiding citizen, Officer, and you can't—"

"That's it! Up against the car and spread 'em. Now!"

Marilee stared at the young man, dumbfounded. "Me?"

"Hey, leave the chick alone," Diablo complained.

"She's got no part in this," his friend agreed. "Do you, sweetheart?"

In a startlingly swift motion, the policeman simultaneously shoved Marilee toward his patrol car and kicked one of her legs to the side, so she ended up spread-eagle against the patrol car, just as he'd ordered. Almost as quickly, he frisked her.

She gasped, caught off balance by the sudden invasion of her person. Her face flamed. "What gives you the right—"

"Easy, Marilee," Luke warned under his breath. "The badge gives him the right to do whatever he wants. When his backup gets here, we'll straighten things out."

"But I can't stand here like some criminal. What will people think?"

One side of his mouth quirked in a grin. "They'll probably figure you're the best-looking old lady in the whole Vipers gang."

"Luke...!" she wailed. If she hadn't been so afraid the policeman would do something really awful, like put her in handcuffs, she would have kicked Luke in the shins for teasing her. At the very least she wanted to strangle him for the way his shoulders were shaking with barely controlled laughter. See if she'd try to rescue him again! she thought grimly.

Fortunately, another patrol car arrived, this one with a sergeant who was hopefully older and wiser. As Luke had promised, it didn't take the senior man long to sort things out. Then they were back in Luke's truck on their way to Newellton.

"He *frisked* me, and all you could do was laugh." Arms folded, she sat glaring out the windshield.

"That poor kid was more scared of you than he was of Diablo. The Vipers' women have a wicked reputation. There's nothing they won't do for their men—bite, claw, scratch out a man's eyes."

"Oh, God . . . I'm not part of the Vipers."

"Fortunately, I was able to convince the sergeant you're basically harmless."

She rolled her eyes. "Thanks, 'Spurs,'" she grumbled. "You have the nicest friends."

"Assuming you can overlook a manslaughter conviction or two, and an attitude, Diablo is a decent guy. When you're in the slammer, you need friends like him."

A shiver uncurled down her spine. She wondered what an enemy would look like. "I'll pass. Thanks, anyway."

"I was twenty when they sent me to the joint. As wild as I'd been, inside I was as green as grass. I wouldn't have survived prison without him."

The thought of how Luke might have been victimized without the protection of someone like Diablo made her skin crawl. Her exile in Los Angeles seemed easy by comparison.

By the time they got back to Newellton, Hawk was already home and stretched out on the couch, bouncing his daughter on his stomach. Beth was making dinner.

"Good news," Marilee announced. She bent over to give Sarah a kiss. "We know for sure who the culprit was in the hit-and-run."

Hawk's eyebrows shot up. "Yeah?" He levered himself to a sitting position, Sarah continuing her deep knee bends on his legs without missing a beat.

"Andy Martins confessed to his grandfather," Luke said. "He's the one who stole the car and ran over Joanie Tarkington."

Hawk reacted to the statement with a frown. "According to the files, the boy was questioned, but he had an alibi. He was home all night."

"His parents lied." Marilee sat down beside Hawk and stretched out her arms to Sarah. The baby shook her head and dived into the safety of Hawk's chest. "Oh, you..." Marilee laughed, remembering how good it felt to have her own child in her arms. In that secret part of herself she seldom acknowledged, she admitted how much she'd like to have a baby she and Luke had created together.

Luke sat down on the edge of the coffee table. "Jake says he'll make a statement if you'll go by the hospital."

"Hospital?"

After they brought Hawk up to date on Jake's heart attack, the sheriff asked, "Did anyone else hear Jake tell you about his grandson?"

"No, I don't think so. Why?" Luke asked.

Hawk handed the baby to Marilee, then stood. "Jake's statement is only hearsay at this point, which doesn't carry a lot of weight."

"I was a witness," Marilee said.

"The problem is you two are..." Hawk glanced from one to the other as though searching for a word "...friends. If something happens to prevent Jake from repeating his story to me or to some other objective observer, your word, Marilee, might not be considered credible."

"I'd never lie."

"On a personal level, I'm willing to believe that. But as an officer of the court..." He let the statement dangle.

"Maybe you ought to get over to the hospital now," Luke suggested. His brows had lowered into a troubled line.

Hawk checked his watch. "I'll call first, see if they'll let me in. I may need his doctor's permission to question Jake and should probably have an attorney present. Sounds like he may be an accessory after the fact."

Marilee had a troubling feeling that the ponderous wheels of justice might move too slowly now, just as they'd moved too quickly when an innocent man had been convicted eight years ago.

* * *

If Isabelle Franklin had been on General Custer's staff, he wouldn't have lost the Battle of Little Big Horn.

She'd outmaneuvered her husband in less than twenty-four hours and had successfully completed a clandestine operation on Marilee by contacting Glen directly. Marilee resented that, but there was little she could do to counter the woman's moves. Besides, Glen had a right to meet his paternal grandparents if that's what he wanted.

"I thought you might like to see Bud's scrapbook from when he was a little boy." Mrs. Franklin ushered Glen toward the kitchen of her restored turn-of-the century home, which was filled with exquisite antiques. "I've got soft drinks and cookies, too, if you'd like."

"Yeah, sure." With an adolescent shrug, he tagged along behind his grandmother.

Marilee eyed Taylor. He looked as uncomfortable with the situation as she felt. "I'll go take a look, too," she said.

He cleared his throat. "Issy misses her grandchildren."

"I can understand that."

"I don't want you to think we're admitting—"

"Mr. Franklin, Glen and I have gotten along fine without you for thirteen years. I'm not going to start suing now about paternity, nor am I going to run around town trying to ruin your reputation. Or Bud's. This meeting was your wife's idea, not mine."

Using a handkerchief, he wiped at the beads of perspiration on his forehead. In the process, he shifted his toupee slightly off kilter. "As long as we understand each other."

Turning her back on Taylor Franklin, Marilee followed her son into the kitchen.

"That's Bud with his first rabbit," Mrs. Franklin said, the tips of her fingers trembling slightly as she caressed a scrapbook photo. "He was about six then, I think. He always loved animals. Was forever bringing home injured birds, not that his father approved."

"Once I found a cat who'd been hit by a car," Glen said. "Mom took him to the vet for me. But he died."

Marilee remembered—an emaciated, bloodied cat and an inconsolable son who'd prayed every night for months for a creature he'd tried to save. The memory brought sudden tears to her eyes. Bud would have done the same.

"Do you have pets?" Mrs. Franklin asked, her eagerness to connect with her grandson palpable.

"No, ma'am. Mom says it's too hard on the animals when you live in an apartment. And we don't have much money...."

Feeling defensive, Marilee said, "Maybe in Helena we can find a house to rent that would allow a dog."

He grinned at her. "A big one?"

"We'll negotiate when the time comes. And he'll be *your* responsibility."

Mrs. Franklin covered Glen's hand with her own. "I'm glad you like animals. Your father..." She looked back at the scrapbook, a sheen of tears in her eyes.

Bud at a Little League game. "I'm afraid he struck out more times than he hit the ball. His teammates elected him captain anyway."

Bud, still chubby before he got his adolescent spurt of growth, with a trumpet in his hand. "His music teacher assured my son he was tone deaf, but Bud arranged for the band to play for a Fourth of July parade in Butte. That was the first time any musical group from Newellton had played outside of our own town. Everyone was very proud of what he had done."

And so the stories went—Bud never quite accomplishing what his parents might have wanted, but still seen as special in his mother's eyes. Through her, Glen caught a glimpse of his father that Marilee couldn't have provided. Nor had she as a seventeen-year-old fully appreciated the true goodness that was in the adolescent who had fathered her child.

"Taylor, dear, wasn't there something you were going to discuss with Marilee?" Mrs. Franklin said as she finally provided the promised soft drinks and cookies.

"Well, yes, ah... There's nothing definite, you understand." He helped himself to a cookie.

"Go ahead, dear."

"It's possible... that is, Newellton is growing." He cleared his throat in his most mayoral manner and locked his hands behind his back like an overweight centurion at parade rest. "We're considering hiring a city manager, someone with planning experience. Of course, we won't be able to pay much initially. Little more than a part-time salary. Tight budgets, you know."

Marilee stared at him incredulously. She'd had nearly ten years of planning experience in one of the biggest cities in the country. That's how she'd landed the job in Helena. "Are you offering me a job here?"

"No, no. Can't do that. We have to hire the most-qualified person. All on the up and up, you know," he blustered, as if Newellton wasn't already a hotbed of nepotism. "But it's legitimate to show some preference to local people. Folks who were raised in Newellton and understand our problems."

"I've been gone for fourteen years. I'd hardly know what the local issues are."

His jowls took on a red glow. "Tried to tell Issy that but she wouldn't listen."

"I also need a full-time job to support my son." Marilee shook her head. "I don't really think I'd be interested." She couldn't imagine living in the town where everyone knew exactly who she'd been and what she'd done. Among other concerns, it wouldn't be fair to her son.

When they finally left the Franklin home—with promises to keep in touch—Glen was in good spirits.

"Hey, my father was okay, wasn't he?"

"Yes, honey." Marilee looped her arm around his shoulders as the press of tears burned once again at the back of her eyes. "I used to think, if things had been different, that your father and I would have made it together even though we were terribly young. But that didn't happen...."

"It's all right, Mom. I understand. And I'm glad I got to meet Isabelle. Even ol' Mr. Franklin. They're not so bad."

She cupped his cheek, so soft and youthful. Tears filled her throat like knotted memories she was finally willing to let go of.

"I love you, Glen Haggerty. I think your father would have been very proud of you."

Chapter Nine

Feeling more than a little anxious about her date with Luke, Marilee entered the living room to greet him. Her son's approving whistle stopped her cold, and heat flooded her face.

"Geez, Mom. You look . . . wow!"

After taking in her appearance with a slow, appraising gaze that did something hot and wild to Marilee's insides, Luke said, "The kid's right. Wow!" He gave a low, intimate sigh.

Marilee swallowed hard. "You look pretty spiffy yourself, Mr. Spurwood." Dynamite sexy was closer to the truth. His elegant, Western-style suit emphasized broad shoulders and lean hips, the silver-blue color darkened his pewter eyes almost to black. He wore a string tie with a fleck of turquoise in the silver bolo, and his boots were the finest leather. "To buy all that you must have robbed a bank."

He grinned. "Sold off a couple of calves for folding money." Extending his hand, he said, "Let's go. We've given the youngster enough of a show for now." He winked at Glen.

Lord, she'd entirely forgotten her son was standing there. Or that Beth was right behind her. She'd only had eyes for Luke. That wasn't like her at all.

Picking up her coat, he helped her slip it on. His breath was warm across her cheek, and she caught the scent of peppermint mixing with his spicy aftershave. Sweet and kissable.

He lifted her hair above her collar—she'd left it brushed out long this evening—and his fingers lingered at the back of her neck. A warm shimmer of longing sped down her spine. Her heartbeat turned erratic, her legs strangely weak. How many years had it been since she'd felt this way? How many years since she'd even had a date?

"Have a good time, Mother," Glen chimed as they went out the door.

Little wonder she hadn't dated since she couldn't remember when. What woman would feel comfortable under the watchful eye of her teenage son?

She, not Luke, was the one who needed to be reminded to be on her best behavior.

By combining wardrobes, Marilee had found a tunic top of her own to match a pair of Beth's tight pants. A colorful scarf and dangling gold earrings completed an outfit that seemed acceptable for any restaurant the rural Montana county had to offer.

There was no excuse at all to feel so nervous. But her uneasy stomach had its own ideas, and she doubted it was because of the meal she'd soon be eating.

"Are you sure the timing's right for us to be celebrating?" she asked as Luke walked her to his truck. "Maybe we should wait until we're sure Jake has cleared your name." Maybe she should wait until she was old enough not to want things she couldn't have. Another hundred years or so ought to be about right.

"I've been waiting for a long time for this night, Marilee." He cupped her elbow to help her into the truck. "I only wish I could have afforded a fancy limo to take us tonight."

"Your truck is fine." The dings and bent fenders didn't matter. In fact, as the two of them got underway and the reflecting lights lining the highway flashed by, Marilee felt like she was traveling on a magic carpet. Determinedly, she fought to remember that she and Luke had no future together.

"What's the first day of a Roman month?" he asked.

"Huh?" She swiveled her head. Perhaps it was the enticing scent of his after-shave filling the truck's cab that had her muddled.

"Seven letters. There's a *d* in it."

"Oh." Shifting mental gears, she let possibilities scroll through her mind. *"Calends,"* she decided. "You count backward from calends to the ides."

"Darn." He struck his palm against the steering wheel. "I should have known that. How 'bout 'chipping away'?"

"What is this? A test?" Passing headlights caught the teasing challenge in his eyes. "How many letters?"

"Five."

"No more hints?"

"I thought you were a topnotch player."

She jammed a playful elbow into his ribs. "*Spall*. How's that?"

A smile played at the corner of his lips. "I think it'll work."

He kept trying to stump her, each answer getting more difficult, the clues less telling, until she was guessing wildly at words, simply because he wouldn't give her half a chance. And because she was laughing so hard.

"See, I knew I was better at crosswords than you." He wheeled into the parking lot next to the restaurant.

"Better?" she complained, laughing again. "You made up the clues, for heaven's sake. You already knew the answers."

"A guy's got to take advantage whenever he has a chance."

"Does that apply only to women? Or are you democratic about who you cheat?"

He eyed her from beneath hooded lids before he switched off the ignition. "I never cheat. And if I hadn't already promised to be on my best behavior... trust me, sweetheart, I'd be first in line to take advantage of you."

His sexual innuendo set off an electrical dance in Marilee's midsection. Surely she'd never be able to swallow a bite of dinner.

Once seated in the restaurant, Luke ordered a dry, white wine. The first sip made Marilee feel instantly intoxicated. Or perhaps another emotion was making her feel light-headed.

One she didn't want to examine too closely.

Luke lifted his glass to Marilee. In the candlelight her eyes sparkled with flecks of gold surrounded by emerald green, and high color rode her sculpted cheeks. Her laughter had a crystalline character, her smile a special warmth that hinted at the pleasure of cozy nights spent in front of a fire or lazy mornings beneath a heavy quilt. Together.

After Luke's eight years of abstinence, his hunger for a steak didn't compare to his hunger for Marilee. He wanted to taste her savory flavor, her warm, sweet juices, and nibble at tender places while together they explored a full range of sensual delights—delicately seasoned pleasures with just the right combination of spice. He wondered if she preferred hot salsa or milder variations on the same theme.

The word games they'd played in the truck had been a sham, an effort to distract himself from thoughts of words like *intimacy, carnal,* and *consummation.*

It hadn't worked.

He knew ex-cons weren't often dealt winning hands in the high-stakes game of life. He was going to lose. Big-time. Just when he'd thought Jake's revelation would get him home free, along came the realtor—that very afternoon—to yank the rug out from under his plans for the future.

Luke didn't want to drag anyone down with him. Especially not a woman like Marilee. She deserved the best of everything—both wine and the man she hooked up with. For tonight he could manage the vintage wine. Then he'd be played out. No reserves. No future.

"Don't leave me now," she said from across the table, her voice a soft caress so filled with caring it was as if she had actually stroked her hands across his flesh.

He blinked and suppressed a curse. "I'm not going anywhere." He couldn't. He was stuck as securely as if he'd stepped into a vat of Super Glue.

"You looked like you'd drifted off to some bad place."

"Sorry." He glanced down at the menu so she couldn't see the disappointment in his eyes. It wasn't enough to want something so much it hurt. That didn't make dreams come true.

He scanned the list of entrees. "I'm going to have a steak, the thickest, juiciest one they've got, black on the outside and red in the middle. I've been dreaming about this night for eight years." Not the biggest dream he'd had, but the only one that was attainable.

She covered his hand with her own. "What's wrong?"

Curling his fingers around hers, he said, "This is a night to celebrate. Jake's going to clear my name. What more could I ask?"

"You tell me."

"Guess I'm not a very good actor." He mentally cursed again, his thumb rubbing the smooth polish on the tips of her fingernails. "The real-estate guy checked the bank records. I'd be lucky to sell the ranch for the debt on it. It seems Dad still owed a bundle after refinancing a few years back. Then, when he died, I agreed to have the bank manage the place for a fee until I got out of prison and could get a handle on things. They ran up quite a bill and claimed it was standard operating procedure."

A frown puckered her forehead. "Does that mean you can't sell the place and use the proceeds to buy the garage you've always wanted?"

"You got it. I have a roof over my head, a few beef and that's it. I can either walk away with no change in my pockets or stick around and try to make the ranch pay. Hell of a choice for a guy who prefers grease over manure, eh?" He nearly choked on a forced laugh.

"Maybe you could set up a garage in your barn."

"The ranch is a long way out of town. I don't see why anyone would want to drive that far when Jake's shop is right in town."

"You think he'll go back to running the business after he's out of the hospital?"

"Maybe he'll sell it or give it to one of his children. It's a prime location with a good customer base."

"How much would it cost to buy him out?"

"More than I've got. Which means I'm stuck in Newellton doing exactly what my old man did—trying to raise cattle on marginal land."

"Maybe you'll discover oil on your property."

Twisting his lips in a wry smile, he said, "I'll drink to that." He tipped his glass, then looked around for the waiter. If only it was as easy to order a break or two when you were down on your luck, Luke could be a happy man. All he wanted was a woman beside him, a future with promise and a past that didn't drag him down into the muck. He tried to keep the bitterness at bay, even knowing the cards were stacked against him.

"Enough of my troubles," he said. "Tell me about your day."

"Glen met his grandparents today."

"Oh, yeah? How'd that go?"

"Pretty well, I guess. Taylor Franklin all but offered me a job here in Newellton."

"You're kidding!"

"Nope. His wife put him up to it, of course. She's a pretty impressive lady, who has her husband wrapped around her little finger."

"So what did you say?"

"I told him no. Like you, there's no way I want to stay in Newellton. Even if the job paid a decent wage—which it doesn't—I figure the townspeople could never forget my reputation."

"That's why you ran away in the first place, right?"

"It's not a whole lot of fun to have people sniggering about you behind your back. When you walk into a room, everyone goes deathly quiet. Or worse, they find someplace they have to go in a hurry."

She fussed with the spoon and knife, arranging them carefully beside her plate and wishing her life could be so easily put in order. If the shame of an unintended pregnancy hadn't driven her out of Newellton, she might have been willing to face down her old reputation. But she had her son to think about. He didn't deserve to live with the burden of her past.

"Then, as soon as they're out of sight," she continued, "you hear giggling, and you know the joke's on you." She didn't want to make Glen suffer the brunt of laughter meant for her.

"It can't have been all that much easier in L.A. for a pregnant young woman alone."

"It could have been disastrous," she admitted. "I had a small savings account, which I cleaned out before I left home. I thought I was in fat city, with a couple of hundred bucks in my pocket after buying bus fare. The first time I tried to rent an apartment, I got a reality check. Job hunting with no skills and no high-school diploma was another eye-opening experience. I was about fifteen minutes from living on the streets when somebody told me about a home for unwed mothers. It was my salvation in more ways than one." It had offered a safe place to stay, encouragement, a chance to get her GED and, finally, connections that led to a decent job.

"I wish I'd been there to help you."

She smiled at him, thinking she could have used a full-fledged hero during those first few years after Glen's birth. "If I've got it figured right, you were just starting high school about the time I dropped out. Assuming I hadn't run away from home, I would have had to baby-sit you."

He raised a skeptical brow. "Trust me, Marilee. I had plenty of adult ideas long before I entered high school. Young or not, I would have considered them all where you were concerned.''

Heat suffused her face and weighted her breasts. ''Regretfully, I seem to have that effect on men.''

''What's wrong with a guy thinking you're sexy? And getting ideas about what he'd like to do with you? I'd think you'd be flattered.''

He honestly didn't get it. Most men didn't.

''Men look at my face, maybe my hair color, then let their gaze slip a little lower, and they never look back. They haven't a clue about who I am or what I want out of life. All they know is that I have big boobs.''

''Maybe you aren't giving us male types enough credit. I know you're a terrific lady who's trying to make a good life for your son and doing a damn good job of it. The fact that I'd like to take you home and make love to you the rest of the night doesn't mean I don't value you as a person.''

''I don't know how to react to that kind of a statement.'' Her body, however, had instantly seized on his idea of making love, responding with an accelerated pulse and a clenching sensation low in her torso. ''I'm not exactly comfortable dealing with men on an intimate level.''

''Because you got burned by Glen's father?''

''That experience certainly made me question my behavior with men. I decided it was a lot safer to keep my distance. That way I couldn't get myself into any more trouble.''

''Sounds boring to me.''

It was. Deadly dull. But no one made snide remarks behind her back. Both she and her son were protected from thoughtless insults and innuendos. That's how she'd arranged her life for the last fourteen years.

As she gazed across the table into Luke's dark eyes, she wondered if she ought to reevaluate her decision to avoid intimate relationships with men. Perhaps there was room for one exception to her self-imposed rule.

But not in Newellton, she realized with a wrenching sense of regret. She couldn't risk more gossip in a town that had already witnessed her downfall. She simply wasn't brave enough to face them down.

The waiter finally returned to take their orders—a rare steak for Luke and veal in a creamy wine sauce for Marilee. During the meal they spoke of ordinary things—her plans for house hunting in Helena, the outcome of a high-profile jury trial, the merits of professional football or if indeed there were any merits to the sport at all.

They laughed together and conversation never lagged.

But Marilee scrupulously avoided discussing what was really on her mind—how Luke's lips would feel pressed against hers, if the wine would taste differently when mixed with the sweet flavor of his tongue, how much she would like to be held in his strong arms and renounce the vow of celibacy she had made so many years ago.

They lingered over cappuccino until they were the last patrons left in the restaurant. But when they got back to Newellton, the lights were on in Hawk's house and the sheriff's car was parked at an odd angle, as though he'd been in a hurry to get into the house.

Luke felt anxiety crawl along his spine.

"Do Beth and Hawk usually stay up so late?" he asked. It was one thing to leave a porch light on for Marilee. This looked like no one was even considering hitting the sack. Which effectively eliminated the kiss at the door Luke had promised himself. He'd been on his best behavior all evening. He figured he deserved a reward, but it didn't seem like it was going to happen the way he had imagined—a kiss that was hot, wet and long.

"A family with an early rising baby rarely stays up late enough to see the eleven o'clock news," Marilee sounded worried. "Maybe something's happened to Sarah. She seemed fine when I left...."

Like a kid who'd suddenly realized there was no Santa Claus, Luke sensed that trouble was coming. Very likely coming in his direction.

"Jake died."

Hawk's announcement as they walked into the house struck Luke like a blow to his gut. "When?"

"About an hour ago."

"Damn!" Luke swallowed a few other well-chosen words not at all suited for polite company, expressions he'd picked up in prison. "Did he talk? Did he have a chance to tell you that Andy was the one who stole the car and ran over that girl?"

Shaking his head, Hawk paced across the living room and tossed his Stetson onto an end table, then shrugged out of his jacket. It didn't look like he'd been home long. "I'd been trying to get in to see him. He drifted in and out of consciousness all day, and the doctor didn't want him disturbed."

A sick knot of disappointment and pain rose up to fill Luke's throat; tension pulled every muscle in his body as taut as a high wire. He needed to go pump iron, to ease the frustrated fury that had him teetering near the brink of explosive release. Eight years in prison had taught him not to let go. But it hurt. Like hell.

"He said he'd take care of things," Luke said. The news was like a switchblade slicing into him. "Maybe he talked to one of the nurses."

"Not about the accident. I checked."

Marilee draped her coat over the back of a chair. She could see what Hawk's announcement was costing Luke in self-control. A muscle ticked in his jaw, his neck was corded with tension and his fingers flexed time and again into fists. He wanted to hit someone, but she knew he wouldn't. However dangerous he might appear, at heart he was a gentle man.

"I can still stand as witness to the fact that Jake pointed the finger at his grandson," she said in an effort to salvage the situation. "Luke can still reopen his case. Surely a judge would believe—"

"Why don't you tell me exactly what Jake said?" Hawk asked. He leveled a gaze at her in a way that left no doubt about his skills as an interrogating officer.

"Well..." She searched her memory, recalling the hospital smells and the oppressive quiet of the intensive-care unit. "First Jake apologized for doing Luke a disservice and said he should have spoken up years ago.''

"Okay.'' Hawk nodded, encouraging her to continue.

"Then he talked about how much he loved Andy.'' To jog her memory, Marilee shot Luke a glance. He was pacing to the fireplace and back, reminding her of a man who was used to being caged in small places. A desperate man. "Oh, yes—then he said he'd be willing to talk to you, Hawk. That you'd understand.''

"And?'' Hawk persisted.

"And...that's it. It was obvious to me Jake was admitting that Andy had stolen the car and was behind the wheel when the hit-and-run happened.''

A frown pressed Hawk's brows into a solid line. "Did he actually say those exact words?''

"Well, no,'' Marilee admitted, "but that's what he meant.''

The sheriff shook his head.

"We both heard him,'' Luke insisted.

"I was there, Hawk. I know what was said,'' she insisted.

"I'm sorry, Marilee. If Luke tried to reopen his case, I doubt a judge would even admit your testimony in court. First of all, it's hearsay. Beyond that, Jake didn't actually make any kind of a statement about Andy's guilt.'' Unbuttoning the cuff of his shirt, Hawk rolled up his sleeve. "Sounds to me like you both heard what you wanted to hear.''

"But that means Luke still can't clear his name,'' she protested. The unfairness of the situation nearly made her physically ill. He was innocent. Why couldn't everyone see that?

Her chin trembled and she fought back the threat of tears. Had she really not heard Jake implicate Andy? She'd been so sure... Other people might doubt Luke's innocence, but she didn't. He had already become so important to her that she had no choice but to believe he was a good man. A man wrongly accused of a crime he hadn't committed.

With a start, she wondered how she had come to feel so strongly about Luke in such a short time. She checked his rugged profile, his evening whiskers beginning to darken his strong jaw, and saw the gentle man he so often masked. Had her feelings for him arrived fully born when he'd pulled her son from the icy pond? Or had they grown more slowly, like filling in the blanks of a crossword puzzle one word at a time?

And now that she realized how much she cared, how would she be able to walk away? Yet she didn't have the courage to face living anywhere within a hundred miles of Newellton. Luke's ranch was well inside that circle.

Luke speared his fingers through his hair. The living room felt crowded, as if the walls were closing in on him. As if he was back in a seven-by-nine-foot cell, with the stink of urine and sweaty bodies, and he'd never get out again.

Fear filled his chest, driving the air from his lungs. He swallowed hard. "Where does that leave me with the robbery?" he asked.

"The folks in Harlowton aren't interested in pursuing the case." Hawk rolled up his other shirtsleeve.

Even relaxed, he looked precision pressed, like a man who had his act together. "The victim died a couple of years ago. Without an eyewitness, they'd have no case."

So no one was set on railroading him back into prison. This time. Luke ought to feel relieved. But as an ex-con, he'd always be suspect. Somebody would stub his toe and they'd dial his number. He'd heard enough stories inside to know a man with a record could expect to get rousted when any crime went down in the vicinity.

Hell, the cops could pull him in for spitting on the sidewalk! He needed to get as far away from Newellton as he could. The other side of the world would be about right.

He slid Marilee a glance. She looked pale. Troubled. He wondered if she'd be willing to go with him, maybe back to L.A. Or to the Deep South. He'd heard the economy there was growing. An auto mechanic might be able to make a living.

Then he remembered the dismal state of his finances. Both she and Glen deserved more than he'd ever have to offer.

Hawk settled a hip on the back of the couch. "Jake may not have made any statement you can use in court about the hit-and-run, but he did something else that speaks volumes about your innocence. At least, to me it does."

Luke shifted his attention back to the sheriff. "What's that?"

"He dictated a codicil to his will to one of the nurses." Hawk handed Luke a single sheet of paper.

"He had enough presence of mind to have two nurses witness his signature. From what they say, he was entirely aware of what he was doing. I think he must have known he was going to die and wanted to make amends for his grandson. But my conjecture wouldn't stand up in court any better than Marilee's testimony."

Luke stared down at the paper. Except for the shaky signature at the bottom, the words were printed neatly in a feminine hand.

Raising his gaze to the sheriff, he asked, "Is this legal?"

Marilee moved closer to Luke and read over his shoulder. Her delicately scented floral perfume had been driving him crazy all night. It still was, but he couldn't think about that now.

"Since his heirs are specifically named with small bequests—with the notable exception of Andy—I believe the will would stand up to any challenge in court," Hawk said. "I also suspect, since Andy's parents evidently lied for him, that they wouldn't be eager to make waves under the circumstances. They might even be grateful to have their consciences eased."

"He left me his garage?"

"The property, building, tools, equipment and inventory. You own Jake's Garage lock, stock and barrel. The whole ball of wax. Or you will as soon as probate closes."

"That has to be the biggest part of Jake's estate," Marilee commented.

Incredulity played around the edges of Luke's brain. Nobody gave away something as valuable as Jake's Garage to someone who wasn't even a relative. Hell, in his whole life, nobody in Newellton had given him anything except grief. "What's this last paragraph about?"

"That proviso is a little unusual," Hawk said, "but I still think it will stand up in court."

"You mean in order to own the garage outright, I've got to operate it for a full year? If I don't, it will be sold off and the proceeds will be distributed among Jake's other heirs?"

"Unusual clause, I admit."

"Why did he do that?" Marilee asked.

Luke wondered the same thing. If Jake had willed him the garage outright, he could have sold it and moved on. But no. His old boss had effectively chained him to Newellton for at least a year. And nowhere had Jake confessed that Luke was innocent of causing Joanie Tarkington's death.

He bristled at the catch-22 the old mechanic had created for him—a new prison, this one without walls. "What the hell made Jake think any of the locals would bring their cars in for repairs with me running the shop, an ex-con accused of killing one of their own?" he asked. "Half the people in town would probably still like to see me strung up."

"Maybe he had more faith in the good folks of Newellton than you do."

"I don't get your meaning."

Hawk folded his arms across his chest. "I suspect when the locals learn about this will, they'll be able to figure out that Jake was saying you hadn't done anything all that bad. They may be a little tentative at first, but I imagine most people will bring in their cars for repairs just like they did with Jake. It'll be up to you to keep their trade."

"Sounds like a hard sell to me."

"Your choice." Hawk shoved himself away from the couch. "I gotta hit the sack. Sarah is worse than a rooster when it comes to waking everyone at dawn. I'm glad I caught you tonight to give you the news instead of having to drive out to your place tomorrow."

"Yeah. Great way to end the evening." Winning a lottery would have been better. Taking Marilee to bed would have topped that by a long shot.

Marilee waited until Hawk left the room before she asked, "What are you going to do?"

He shrugged, though the gesture felt awkward. Almost painful. "There isn't any choice. Not really. I've got a ranch I can't sell and I just acquired a garage that's in the same boat. If I walk away, I've got squat. *Nada.* The only thing I can do is hang on for at least a year. Then maybe..."

By then it would be too late for him and Marilee. She'd be long gone to Helena. No way would she stick around while he tried to dig out from under the pile of manure that had been dumped on him.

No woman in her right mind would.

Chapter Ten

He'd withdrawn from her.

It had been a week since Marilee had seen Luke. She'd called him once, but to say he'd been abrupt on the phone was an understatement. She mourned his absence just as she had felt the loss when her father had died.

And when Bud had left her, however unwillingly, when she'd needed him most.

Only Glen was welcome in Luke's life. Almost every day her son slipped out to see him, using Hawk's bike to cover a distance Marilee wasn't invited to travel.

She had become persona non grata, a mere blip in a dangerous man's past. It was better that way, she told herself—a blatant lie she desperately wanted to believe.

Unfortunately, whatever she might feel didn't change the fact that when she drove her car for any distance, ugly blue smoke billowed out the back. Either her transmission had turned to confetti and was spewing oil or the installation of the new oil pan had been faulty.

It was almost time for Marilee to leave for Helena. The month she had allowed for her visit with Beth had nearly passed. She had a job waiting for her. A future. A new home to create for herself and her son.

She didn't dare set off to drive that far without knowing her car would make it and not leave her stranded, at the mercy of whoever might stop to help. Heroes like Luke Spurwood weren't waiting along every county road.

Standing next to her car in front of Jake's Garage and watching Luke poke around under the hood of the one car in for repairs, she felt decidedly ill at ease. Evidently Jake's heirs had agreed to let Luke run the garage until probate closed. What could she say to him? How could she even hint she'd like to stay?

Which would be foolhardy beyond belief.

Marilee didn't belong in Newellton. She never had. Even now she could feel the press of Myrtle Symington's eyes on her from across the street at the grocery store, all but physically shoving her out of town. When two women walked by, talking in hushed tones, Marilee's ears burned. Were they gossiping about her? she wondered, trying not to let it matter.

Luke lifted his head and spotted her waiting. For an instant she saw unadulterated longing in his eyes, then his expression grew closed. His hooded, wary look chilled the hollow spot in her chest where her heart should have been, a part of her she had evidently misplaced somewhere along a snowy county road en route to Newellton.

He looked every bit a maverick. A rebellious lock of hair had slid across his forehead, his jaw was dark and rough with day-old whiskers that would leave burns on a woman's sensitive skin if he kissed her. Beneath his eyes he had the bruised look of someone who hadn't been sleeping well. A mirror image of the damage done by her own restless nights, she imagined.

Wiping his hands on a grease-smudged rag, he nodded and said, "Something I can do for you?"

Turn back the clock, she almost said. To a time when neither one of them had reputations to live down. To a place where being together wouldn't put Glen in jeopardy of having to fight his way home from school every day. But there was no way Luke could make those kinds of repairs to their lives.

She tried to concentrate on the one thing he could fix.

"Smoke." Her voice caught in her throat. "My car spews blue smoke when I get up to speed."

He frowned. "Let's get it up on the hoist. I'll take a look."

They both reached for the car door at once. His hand covered hers on the handle, big and strong and ruggedly textured. She gritted her teeth against the achingly pleasurable sensation.

He pulled away as though he'd been burned. "Sorry. You drive and I'll direct you."

"Okay." It wasn't okay. The whole situation was desperately, hopelessly wrong, and there wasn't a thing Marilee could do to change it.

Her hand trembled as she switched on the ignition.

Following his gestures, she drove into the garage, amid hoists and toolboxes and the smell of grease. This was the kind of place Luke wanted to be. Maybe needed to be in order to get his life back on track.

She wished him well. And ached because she wouldn't be there to celebrate his successes. Or encourage him should he fail.

"Okay." He waved. "You can shut it off."

She got out of the car and waited while he raised the lift. The hum of the hydraulic device filled the silence.

Hunching his broad shoulders, he peered under the car, poking at mysterious mechanical parts she'd have no hope of naming in a word puzzle. His old jeans were soft with wear, gloving his buttocks and muscled thighs. She'd never have a chance to touch him intimately, or feel the press of his lean, hard body against hers. His strong arms would never encompass her, offering protection from icy storms that buffeted her life.

"See anything?" she asked, more in hopes of hearing warmth in his voice than in learning the cause of her car trouble.

"Maybe." He reappeared from under the car, gazed at her for a lingering heartbeat, then picked up a power tool. "Looks like Jake didn't get the bolts tightened down enough on the oil pan. The oil leaks out and blows back onto the hot exhaust system. That's what makes it smoke."

"Oh."

"It'll only take a minute to fix."

"Fine." Why did she feel disappointed that the repairs wouldn't take a week—a month—so she'd have an excuse to remain within shouting distance of Luke? Even if he had been avoiding her.

The air wrench screamed, mimicking the primal cry that threatened to rip from Marilee's throat, as Luke tightened the offending bolts. She couldn't give in to the impulse. Luke wasn't right for her. Or for Glen. Not here in Newellton.

Luke finished the job, then pulled on the lever to lower the car. He seemed so cold. So distant. Her heart sank at the same slow, relentless speed as the hoist delivered the car back to ground level.

"Guess you'll be heading out to Helena pretty soon," he said. A muscle ticked in his jaw.

"Our bags are all packed." The brightness of her tone belayed the pain clawing in her chest.

"Tell Glen goodbye for me."

"Thanks for letting him hang around." Marilee would liked to have hung around, too. She could have brought him coffee. Or handed him tools. But that would have caused all kinds of speculation among the locals. And he hadn't wanted her, in any case. "I hope he didn't get in your way too much."

"No problem. He's a good kid."

"Yes." She wanted to place her palm on Luke's cheek, brush back the straying lock of hair from his forehead. She didn't dare. Not now when she was teetering on the brink of tears.

"So I guess it's so long for us, too." His gaze held hers. The embers of passion flickered momentarily in his dark eyes. "If I'm ever in Helena, maybe I'll look you up."

"I'd like that." With force of will, she kept a pleading note from her voice. "You can always get my address and phone number from Beth."

"Yeah. Right. I'll keep that in mind."

He wouldn't call her. Marilee knew that.

Clean breaks were better anyway. That's why she'd left Newellton the first time without saying goodbye. Without any strings attached, people could start over.

Luke wanted to do that.

So did she. Except this time she suspected the empty feeling of loneliness might never go away.

The wrench slipped and Luke cracked the back of his knuckles. He hardly felt the pain.

Marilee had been gone an hour. She was probably cruising down the highway by now. And all he could think about was how he wanted to run his fingers through the silken strands of her flyaway hair one more time. Touch his lips to hers and taste them again. Slide his arms around her, feeling her breasts pressing against his chest. Hear her sigh with pleasure.

But he'd made sure that would never happen again.

He swore and sucked a drop of blood from his knuckle.

Toughing out a year in Newellton would be worse than doing time in solitary. He had two jobs—if you could call them that—and neither one provided enough income to support himself, much less a woman and her kid. Before dawn he handled whatever chores he could manage around the ranch. Then came a full day at the garage, with too damn few customers, followed by an endless evening of more chores that needed doing.

He wouldn't even consider asking a woman to share that kind of life. Not that Marilee would have said yes. She'd made it as clear as a Montana sunrise that she didn't want anything more to do with Newellton. Given her past, he could hardly blame her.

And that's why he'd forced himself to stay away from her this last week.

Turning big rocks into little ones on a chain gang wouldn't have been any harder. Or less painful. Maybe if Jake had exonerated Luke as he'd promised, things would be different. Maybe a year from now...

Hell, a lot of things could happen in the course of twelve long months. He'd do the time, then see.

At the sound of a car coming to a stop in front of the shop, Luke looked up.

He shouldn't have been expecting either a customer or Marilee returning to say she'd changed her mind about the merits of living in Newellton. Still, he couldn't quite quash the wave of disappointment that swept over him when he saw who it was.

"What's up, Hawk?" he asked the sheriff.

"I brought you some county bidding forms."

Luke scowled. "What for?"

"Jake had the contract to do maintenance on the two patrol cars that work this end of the county. I figured you'd want to try for them, too."

"I could sure use the business." He accepted the sheets of paper from Hawk and gave them a quick once-over.

Sliding an appraising look around the nearly empty shop, Hawk said, "Pretty slow, huh?"

"Yeah. Looks like the good folks of Newellton aren't too sure about having an ex-con working on their cars. Probably figure I'll rip off the contents of their glove compartments."

"They'll come around."

"If things don't pick up, I might as well walk away and give the place to Jake's heirs. I won't even be able to pay the electric bill."

Hawk removed his Stetson and smoothed his forearm along the brim. Leaning against the fender of the car Luke had been working on, he folded his arms across his chest. "I was kinda surprised Marilee left today," he said.

At his overly casual tone, Luke straightened. "Why not? She's got a job lined up in Helena. That's why she came back to Montana."

"Funny, she looked to me like she was on her way to her own funeral."

"You mean she was sick?"

"Nope. Not unless you count love as an illness. Granted, the symptoms are pretty darn close—comes on fast and lays you low before you know what's hit you. Not unlike a bad case of the flu, I suppose."

Luke stared incredulously at the spit-and-polish officer of the law. "I think you must have been reading her wrong."

"I might have, but Beth said the same thing. The way I see it, the two of 'em are sisters and pretty much alike—stubborn to the point of distraction and cussedly independent. That makes 'em darn hard on the men who fall for them."

"I don't have any right to—"

"You've had some trouble, Luke. I understand that makes things awkward." Hawk shoved away from the car. "Mind if I make a suggestion?"

Luke shrugged. "Why not?" He was just about tapped out when it came to ideas.

"Kidnap her."

"Come again?"

"If you feel as strongly about Marilee as I think you do, I'd recommend kidnapping her. Find yourself a pony and go after your lady love. Worry about the details later."

Luke suppressed a surprised chuckle. Marilee had told him about the rocky romance between Hawk and his wife. At the last moment, minutes before Beth's scheduled return to her life in New York in the advertising business, the sheriff had finally come to his senses. According to the female version of the story, he'd unbent enough to perform a mock kidnapping of Beth on a neighbor's horse. The fact was, Beth had already decided to stay in Newellton come hell or high water.

"I don't think the same scenario applies to me," Luke said, growing serious again. An ex-con could hardly compare himself to a man who'd won a landslide election victory in the county and had an impeccable reputation. "Marilee has good reasons not to want to live in Newellton."

"So did Beth, or at least she thought she did. Neither of the Haggerty girls got a real good shake from this town the first time around. With Beth, they've done a whole lot better on their second chance. My gut feeling is that'd be true for Marilee, too."

Luke wasn't so sure. Both he and Marilee had a lot of strikes against them. Combined, their pasts would impact heavily on any chance they might have for a future together. And the one who would pay the biggest price might be her son. Luke couldn't handle that kind of guilt.

"It's a helluva long ride on a pony to Helena," he commented.

"Your choice." Hawk extended his hand and Luke realized he was offering friendship in the clasp they shared. "I suspect, for some women, getting kidnapped in an old pickup truck would work just as well."

"I'll think on it."

"Marilee promised to call Beth tonight to let her know where they'll be staying. They don't want to lose touch with each other again."

Neither did Luke. But did he have a right to drag Marilee back to Newellton against her will?

Hawk settled his hat on his head. "Well, be seeing you."

"Right." Unconsciously wiping his hands on the old rag, he said, "If you're in no hurry, maybe you could help me out."

"Sure. What do you need?"

"Nobody's got the combination to Jake's safe. I can drill it open, but I'd like a witness around in case there's money inside or some sort of personal effects. I don't want anyone accusing me of—"

"I understand."

"It won't take long." From the toolbox, Luke retrieved a high-speed, tempered-steel bit and drill. Hawk followed him into the office.

"Doesn't Arletta have the combination?" the sheriff asked.

"Nope. I checked. Jake always opened it for her and got out whatever cash she was going to deposit."

With the bookkeeper's help, Luke had cleaned out most of the clutter in the small office, and she'd taken the invoices and receipts home to sort through.

Kneeling in front of the low, boxy safe, he drilled next to the combination lock. The drill gave a high-pitched whine. Metal filings peeled back from the tip and a wisp of smoke rose, smelling of scorched iron.

When the door swung open, Luke discovered a stack of twenties on the top shelf, maybe a thousand dollars in all. He passed the lot up to Hawk. "Guess this belongs to the family."

"I'll see what the lawyer says."

Beneath the money there was a plain white business envelope on which was written To Whom It May Concern.

Luke lifted the envelope gingerly. A smudge stained the white paper; the handwriting looked unsteady. *I've taken care of things.... It's safe* Jake had promised. Maybe he'd meant it was *in* the safe—Luke's absolution for a crime he hadn't committed.

"Here. Take a look at this." Luke handed Hawk the sealed envelope.

The sheriff studied it a moment, then lifted the flap and slid out a single sheet of paper. He read the handwritten message so darn slowly that Luke was about ready to snatch it away from him and read it himself. He could barely breathe for the amount of hope that was filling his chest.

A future.

A chance to make it here in Newellton. And maybe, just maybe, with Marilee.

Hawk raised his head. Little by little a smile lifted his lips. "This is it, Luke. What you've been looking for. Jake's full admission that his grandson confessed that he was the one who killed Joanie Tarkington. I'd say, when we put this in the hands of a judge, you'll be completely exonerated. Congratulations!''

"I'm cleared?''

"Close enough. I'll put out a wanted bulletin on Andy, not that I think it will do much good. But if he ever turns up again, he'll have to answer a lot of questions.''

Grown men didn't cry. Sure as hell, ex-cons weren't likely to shed any tears.

So Luke wiped his eyes with the back of his hand and swallowed thickly. After eight long years, the waiting was over. Jake had kept his promise.

The silver ribbon of highway slid beneath Marilee's car in a blur of speed. She wanted to get to Helena as fast as possible, so she drove with a heavy foot on the accelerator, as though she could outrun thoughts of Luke. Concentrating on the road provided the only barrier against the tears that threatened to overflow her heart.

Beside her, and oblivious to her emotional turmoil, Glen snapped his fingers and tapped his foot in rhythm to unheard music playing through his earphones. Marilee wished she were as easily distracted.

The bruise on Glen's cheek had faded nicely. The bruises on Marilee's psyche, left there by Luke's emotional withdrawal, would take far longer to heal.

"Hey, Mom," Glen said, slipping off his electronic ears. "Is that the state pen where Luke was in jail?''

Instinctively, Marilee slowed and let her gaze follow Glen's off the side of the highway toward the prison. The imposing brick walls looked bleak, the guard towers every few hundred feet threatening exclamation points. The thought of Luke locked inside that fortress for eight long years knotted her stomach painfully. An innocent man. How had he survived? He'd deserved so much better.

Pensive, Glen said, "Luke told me how tough it was inside. He said I'd better keep my nose clean and stick with school. Not that he figured I was planning on doing anything all that bad. He just wanted to warn me."

She blessed Luke's concern and guidance for her impressionable son. "Did you believe him?"

"Yeah." Glen turned toward his mother. "I wish Luke could be my dad. I thought...I mean, you two seemed to be getting along pretty good."

She slowed to a stop along the gravel shoulder. She'd known Glen liked Luke, and wanted a father, but perhaps she hadn't fully appreciated how close the two of them had grown. "Luke and I got along fine."

"Then how come you didn't decide to get married?"

"Relationships between men and women aren't always quite that easy, Glen."

"No? Does that mean you don't love Luke?"

A lie thickened in her throat. Like a dose of bitter medicine, she swallowed it down. She'd always been truthful with her son. This was no time to start lying, either to him, or worse, to herself.

"Yes, I love Luke." How could the words feel so right when the truth hurt so much?

"Does he love you?"

"I don't know. He seemed to care...." And then he'd cut her off, left her feeling uncertain, filled with the same insecurities that had taunted her as an adolescent when she'd found herself in trouble. Fears that she was unlovable. That it was her fault somehow that Bud hadn't wanted her then—and Luke didn't now. That her father had died because even God had found her unworthy.

"Then how come, Mom, he's back in Newellton and we're on our way to dumb ol' Helena?"

"That's where my new job is."

"You could get a job in Newellton," Glen announced with a combination of youthful petulance and optimism. "It wouldn't be all that hard."

Actually, a job had practically landed in her lap, courtesy of Taylor Franklin, but that wasn't the point.

"I can't live in Newellton, honey. You know from firsthand experience how much people talk in a small town. I couldn't handle the gossip and neither could you."

"Sure I could."

"You've already taken a beating once. How many more times—"

"I wouldn't listen to what anybody said." He slumped down in his seat in a posture only an adolescent could manage. "Next time, I'd just put on my ears. Then they could say any dumb thing they wanted to and it wouldn't bother me. Not if you and me and Luke could be a family." As if to add emphasis, he snapped his earphones back into place, effectively cutting off any response Marilee might make. "Seems to me you'd be better off if you had some ears, too, so you wouldn't have to listen to anyone you didn't want to hear," he mumbled.

Would that real life were so easy.

She glanced at the imposing presence of the prison. Luke had managed to endure eight years behind those walls. Her self-imposed exile had been much different, but no less difficult to bear, she realized. And they had both been equally innocent.

In her case, adolescent love couldn't be called a crime. She'd carried more than her share of guilt over the years—erroneously. Her grandest accomplishment had been raising Glen, her greatest success the fine young man he was becoming. Lifting her chin, Marilee realized she had a right to be proud of herself and her son. She didn't have to apologize to anyone.

With the same speed as dawn breaking on a prairie horizon, she wondered why she hadn't realized that sooner.

When Luke had left those prison gates, he'd thought he'd be a free man. But through an odd series of good and bad fortune, his choices had become more limited than hers. She was free to go to Helena. He wasn't. In order to assure his future, he had one more year to serve.

And there was nobody in Newellton to stand with him against the taunts and gossip, the unkind remarks that were sure to dog his heels.

She closed her hands tightly around the steering wheel. Nobody had been there when she'd needed them, either.

No, she thought, that wasn't right. Grandma Claire would never have thrown her out. And certainly Beth wouldn't have turned her back when she'd needed a shoulder to cry on.

But Marilee hadn't asked. She'd simply run away.

It followed that a man who had been in prison for eight years wouldn't be looking for a place to cry. Nor would his pride allow him to ask for anyone's help.

With belated wisdom, she understood that Luke had withdrawn emotionally because she'd made her views on Newellton abundantly clear. He was ready to suffer alone rather than ask her to stay.

Damn his hide. He was being a noble hero!

With a quick glance in the rearview mirror, she gunned the engine and made a U-turn, bumping across the weed-choked divide.

"Geez, Mom! What are you doing?"

"I'm going to go propose to Luke Spurwood." And maybe find them both pairs of earphones so they wouldn't hear anything except words of love. From each other.

"All right, Mom! Way to go!" Glen gave her a high five as they headed back the way they had come.

"He may say no," she warned.

"I don't think so. He was talkin' pretty sappy about you. I think he's got it bad."

Grinning, Marilee hoped her son was right. A proud man was hard to read. Or to convince of what would be best for him. She might well be making the most foolish mistake of her life. And she had a history of making some real doozies.

Chapter Eleven

Luke grabbed the chain to roll the garage door down. Under normal circumstances it'd be too early to close up shop, but business wasn't exactly booming. And if he was going to drive all the way to Helena, he needed to head home and get cleaned up, as well as bed down the horses for the night.

Besides, he was so damn excited he probably wouldn't be able to do a decent job of changing a tire if his life depended on it.

Before he got the door all the way shut, a car pulled up in front of the shop.

Marilee's car.

Luke had an instant attack of nerves. Hell, he'd planned to think about what he wanted to say during the drive to Helena. Maybe even rehearse the words out loud—how they could work it out. A year wasn't all that long—not for a man who'd spent eight long ones in the slammer.

A man who could finally put his past behind him.

Her arrival had shoved every coherent thought right out of his head and sent his libido into high gear. Elation and caution warred for dominance in his gut.

"Yo, Luke," Glen called cheerfully as he hopped out of the car. "How's it going?"

"Okay, I guess," he responded uncertainly. He watched Marilee get out of the car, too. She was wearing the same tight-fitting jeans she'd had on earlier in the day and a soft, clingy sweater that invited a man's caress. Her vibrant hair was pulled back in a haphazard ponytail he instantly wanted to release.

He might not deserve Marilee, but that sure as hell didn't stop him from wanting her. Permanently.

"More car trouble?" he asked, relieved that his voice sounded even, as if his excitement and nerves were under control. Which they weren't.

"Not exactly."

He raised his eyebrows. "What does that mean?"

"It means..." Fiddling with her car keys, she glanced at her son. "Did you have somewhere you wanted to go, Glen?"

The kid's elbow rested on the top of the car. "Naw, I don't think so."

"Yes, Glen," she said with a surprising touch of sternness as color rose to her cheeks. "I'm sure you said you were going to check out some new CDs at the record store."

"I did?" He looked confused, and then a big grin split his face. "Yeah, right. I remember now." He gave

Luke a thumbs-up sign. "I'll see you guys later." He turned and jogged off down the street.

Cocking his head, Luke wondered at the odd look Glen had given him. "What was that all about?"

"There's something I wanted to ask you and I thought it would be better if we had a little privacy."

"Privacy?" He glanced around. There weren't many people in sight. A car was parked in front of the grocery store across the street; a woman was just leaving the beauty shop next door. Not exactly Times Square. Maybe he could do some asking himself. "You want to come inside?"

"Yes, that would be a good idea."

Standing in the middle of his shop, Marilee felt awkward and ill at ease. A thousand second thoughts assailed her. Maybe she should have phoned. How would she bear it if he bluntly said he had no interest in marrying her? Worse yet, what if he was *kind* and still sent her packing?

The smell of grease and oil made her slightly sick to her stomach. Her legs felt weak.

"What is it, Marilee?"

"I've been thinking... I mean, Glen and I were talking...." Being tortured with thumbscrews struck her was probably less painful than what she was going through now. She'd never felt more vulnerable. "What if I took that job Taylor Franklin offered?"

"I thought it didn't pay very well."

"It doesn't. But if Glen and I were living at your ranch..."

Luke's brows arched again. A smile played at the corners of his lips.

"...The salary would be enough to put food on the table."

"For three of us?"

"Well, I could put Glen on a diet." She wasn't doing this very well. The words were sticking in her throat, and her tongue was so dry she could hardly speak at all.

"You figure I need to be on a diet, too?"

"Oh, no, you'll need your strength."

His smile grew wider. "Because I'm working two jobs?" The gleam in his dark eyes suggested he was catching on, even if what she was saying wasn't coming out quite right.

"Among other reasons." Her lips curved into a smile that matched his. She imagined they'd spend whatever spare time Luke might have enjoying a variety of sensual activities that would consume a lot of calories. "I promise you'll need all the energy you can muster."

"I like the sound of that." He stepped closer, the inches between them narrowing fractionally. "But the truth is I was planning to drive into Helena tonight and ask you a question or two myself."

"You were?" Her hopes soared.

"Yeah. I was thinking that Helena isn't all that far away. Maybe you and Glen could come here on weekends. That way you could keep your job—"

"No," she blurted. "I've already suffered through too many lonely nights, worked too many crossword puzzles alone because I didn't have anyone to love. I don't want to miss a single night with you, Luke Spurwood. Not a single minute when we could be together."

"Love?"

"Yes," she admitted. Her voice was soft, tentative, filled with fear that he might reject the only real gift she had to offer.

"It would only be for a year or so. I know you don't want to live here in Newellton, but we wouldn't be apart that much." His rough voice was strangely husky as his arms slid around her. He tugged her closer and their bodies gently collided from thigh to chest.

Heat traveled to every sensitive spot where they made contact, then bounced back to curl low in Marilee's body. "A year's too long to be apart. The roads in the winter can be treacherous. You wouldn't want me traveling back and forth."

"You have been known to drive off the road into the ditch occasionally," he conceded.

"Turns out you can meet the nicest people that way." She'd met a dark, dangerous man who was a noble hero at heart.

A chuckle rumbled in Luke's chest. "What about Glen?"

"He needs an every-day father, not just a weekend dad." And she needed an every-day husband, one to hold her and love her as much as she loved him. "There might be a few rough days at first till he makes friends in town, but I think he'll manage fine." She would, too, even if she had to learn to walk around town with her hands over her ears.

But that wouldn't be necessary, she quickly reminded herself. By loving Luke, she'd found a way to discard the unnecessary shame that had been weighing her down. She'd keep her chin held high from now on, no matter what anyone said.

"I suppose that means I'll have to get a satellite dish."

"He might even be willing to negotiate that item."

"That eager, eh?" A kiss whispered across her forehead. "How 'bout his mom? Are you ready to do a little negotiating?"

"What'd you have in mind?"

"I love Glen. He's a really neat kid. But I'd kinda like to have a kid or two of my own. Would you mind...?"

Tears sprang to her eyes. "I can't think of anything more wonderful than to have your child, Luke. I can hardly wait." He hugged her so tightly she wasn't sure she'd ever be able to breathe again.

"You know, sweetheart, I'm not sure if I can make a success of either the ranch or Jake's Garage, but I'll do my damnedest. For you and Glen and, well, any kids that come along. But I do have some good news."

"Nothing else matters as long as we're together.... News?" she echoed, curiosity warring with the thrilling feeling of love given and returned in full measure.

"Jake left a letter in his safe. He admitted everything. That Andy had confessed to the hit-and-run. It had all gone down just as we suspected. Andy was mad at his girl and he was trying to frighten her. He miscalculated. Fatally. Hawk's going to help me reopen my case to present the new evidence."

Tears pooled in Marilee's eyes. "I'm so happy for you."

"The truth is, clearing my name has become less important to me than you are." He groaned and kissed her where the pulse beat wildly at her temple. "Marilee Haggerty, I may be asking you to make the worst mistake of your life. But I love you, and if you don't leave right now, I'm never going to let you go."

She stroked his cheek, cherishing the masculine feel of his dark stubble of whiskers, relishing the determined look in his pewter eyes. "I'm pretty stubborn, Spurwood. There's no more chance of you getting rid of me—now that I know you love me—than there is of the Great Salt Lake icing over in August."

"How'd I get so lucky I managed to find you?"

"Must come from rescuing damsels in distress."

"You'll marry me?"

"Name the day."

As though he couldn't wait any longer, he dipped his head and brushed his mouth against hers. Her lips softened and clung. "I like my kisses hot, wet and wild," he warned.

"Yes," was all she had a chance to utter before he devoured her with a kiss meant to demonstrate that he was a man of his word. His tongue plundered the depths of her mouth. His teeth nibbled on her lower lip, each gentle tug setting up a responding vibration low in her body. She sighed into his mouth and let her tongue duel with his.

Luke's hand slipped beneath her sweater, warm and rough, arousing as he cupped her breast. With his fingertips, he repeated the same sensual tug on her nipple that his teeth had performed on her lip.

Only vaguely, and after some time, did Marilee become aware of a ruckus outside the door to the garage.

"Yoo-hoo! Anybody home?"

Luke groaned. "Lousy timing."

Agreeing with his assessment, Marilee tried to compose herself and straightened her sweater. Her heart was pounding so loudly she imagined Mrs. Russell could hear it from where she was standing.

"There you are, young man." Striding in a spritely manner into the garage, Millie Russell smiled, her huge parrot perched on her shoulder. "I do hope you're still open for the day."

The bird squawked. *"Watch out, fella! We're under attack!"*

Marilee stifled a laugh.

"Yes, ma'am," Luke said, eyeing the bird. "I suppose the shop's still open. If it's an emergency?"

"Well, Sheriff Hawk dropped by. Such a nice man. He told me how it was really Andy who'd killed that poor girl. *Tsk tsk*. What a shame. And Jake keeping the secret all those years. Then the sheriff reminded me how important it is to have the brakes on my car checked regularly. I'd forgotten. I'm so busy, you know, what with my volunteer work for the Heart Association and the Rehab Center. Of course, before my dear Arnold died he used to take care of that sort of thing." She finally stopped chattering to draw a breath.

"Could it wait till tomorrow?" Luke asked.

The parrot appraised Marilee, then gave her a one-eyed wink. *"Hiya, toots!"* he purred.

"It wouldn't usually matter, but I'm off with the garden club tomorrow." Mrs. Russell ignored her talkative pet. "We're going to Helena for a seminar on propagating bromeliads—such a challenge—and I've agreed to drive. Naturally, I wouldn't want to chauffeur my friends if my car isn't safe."

"Yes, ma'am, I can understand that." He shot Marilee a questioning look.

She shrugged. "You can't very well turn a customer away," she said under her breath. "Now that you're going to have a family to support."

Luke grinned at her. "Sorry. We'll take up later where we left off," he promised, in a low voice just as another car arrived.

"Dadburnit!" Taylor Franklin slammed the car door. "That fool sheriff gave me a ticket. Me! The town mayor! Says my taillight's burned out."

"Man overboard!" Charlie hopped from Mrs. Russell's shoulder to an air hose dangling from the ceiling. He swung perilously close to the top of Franklin's head.

Watching in total fascination, Marilee held her breath. What, she wondered, was that bird up to?

"My goodness, it looks like there's a riot going on over here, what with all the cars parked out front. Hawk said your business was really picking up." All eyes shifted toward Myrtle Symington as she walked into the garage. "And well it should, what with you having been sent to jail for a crime you plum had nothing to do with. Hope you can work my car in for a lube job, Luke."

"Would tomorrow be soon enough?" Under his breath, Luke complained to Marilee, "Don't these people know a guy could have more interesting things on his mind than fixing cars?"

"That's what happens to a successful businessman. Work, work, work. Looks like your future brother-in-law has been rounding up customers for you." She slipped her arm through his, knowing she'd never been so happy. The garage was going to be a success under Luke's management. She could feel it in her bones, knew it in her heart. "Why don't I go on home? When you're ready, dinner will be on the table."

"Home?"

"Your place. That four-poster I slept in upstairs has plenty of room for two."

He leaned over to give her a quick kiss. "You can bet I'm going to set a record for how fast brakes can be checked."

"Don't forget the mayor's taillight."

Glancing toward Franklin, Marilee found her gaze being drawn upward. She nudged Luke as, slowly, with the precision of a surgeon, Charlie stretched one foot downward and hooked a single claw into the mayor's hair. Withdrawing it just as carefully, the parrot lifted Taylor Franklin's toupee to his own precarious perch.

"Reef your sails, bucko!"

* * * * *

COMING NEXT MONTH

Take 4 bestselling love stories FREE

Plus get a FREE surprise gift!

Are your lips succulent, impetuous, delicious or racy?

Find out in a very special Valentine's Day promotion—THAT SPECIAL KISS!

Inside four special Harlequin and Silhouette February books are details for THAT SPECIAL KISS! explaining how you can have your lip prints read by a romance expert.

Look for details in the following series books, written by four of Harlequin and Silhouette readers' favorite authors:

Silhouette Intimate Moments #691
Mackenzie's Pleasure by *New York Times* bestselling author Linda Howard

Harlequin Romance #3395
Because of the Baby by Debbie Macomber

Silhouette Desire #979
Megan's Marriage by Annette Broadrick

Harlequin Presents #1793
The One and Only by Carole Mortimer

Fun, romance, four top-selling authors, plus a FREE gift! This is a very special Valentine's Day you won't want to miss! Only from Harlequin and Silhouette.

VAL96

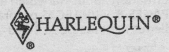

You're About to Become a *Privileged Woman*

Reap the rewards of fabulous free gifts and benefits with proofs-of-purchase from Silhouette and Harlequin books

Pages & Privileges™

It's our way of thanking you for buying our books at your favorite retail stores.

PROOF OF PURCHASE
SR-PP96
Offer expires October 31, 1996

**Harlequin and Silhouette—
the most privileged readers in the world!**

For more information about Harlequin and Silhouette's PAGES & PRIVILEGES program call the Pages & Privileges Benefits Desk: 1-503-794-2499

Silhouette®

SR-PP96